This book is dedicated to John—my brother and best friend.

Acknowledgments

Thank you to my family and friends for their support, humor and indulgence. A special thanks to my chosen sister, Patty, for twenty-five years of laughter. Thank you, Sam, for what you've brought to my life.

Thank you to all the great people at Spinsters Ink, especially Christi Cassidy who is without a doubt the most patient and thorough editor in the world.

About the Author

I never sleep with my windows open at night.
I fear all my dreams will sneak outside and dance in the moonlight.

Dani O'Connor is a dreamer.

SAME SOCKS
marriage

DANI O'CONNOR

Spinsters Ink
2007

Spinsters Ink
P.O. Box 242
Midway, Florida 32343

Printed in the United States of America on acid-free paper
First Edition

Editor: Christi Cassidy
Cover designer: KIARO Creative Ltd.

ISBN-10: 1-883523-86-9
ISBN-13: 978-1-883523-86-2

Chapter One

I met Jules when she was my teaching assistant during her senior year at Central Woman's College. She was passionate about the English language and loved to be the center of attention. The few times she took over the class, she was more of a stand-up comic than a literature teacher. The students loved her, but none as much as Sarah. Sarah was a bright-eyed sophomore who sat in the front row and made heavy puppy eyes every time Jules entered the lecture hall. I used to sit back and observe the innocent flirtation between the two. Eventually it reached a point where the coquetry had Jules so distracted that she couldn't hold a train of thought. That's when I stepped in. I, of course, being the expert on student crushes and gay relations.

"Jules, meet me at Psycho's at four," I whispered between classes, referring to the bar on the other side of campus. "We need to talk about some changes in the syllabus."

Jules looked at her watch and started to make an excuse. The look on my face must have told her something was up. "Sure, Doc. But you're buyin'."

Psycho's was relatively empty for a Friday afternoon. Most of the students had already headed out of town for the weekend. I found a booth in the corner, away from prying ears and gossipy sorority girls. I had a pitcher ready and waiting and resisted the urge to drink the whole thing knowing that Jules would be late. She always told me how she hated driving her truck so would no doubt be walking from her apartment a mile away. I would have offered her a ride, but frankly, I didn't feel like cleaning out my messy car. When she finally arrived, she was red-faced and had a definite sweat moustache. I admit that I felt a little guilty, especially for the embarrassment I was fixin' to cause.

"It's about time. I'm on my third pitcher." I handed her a cold mug and coaster.

"No, you're not. I'm only twenty minutes late. You couldn't drink more than two in twenty minutes." She dabbed her glistening forehead with a bar nap.

"Why don't you just drive, dorko?"

"I hate that truck. I feel like a redneck around here."

"Around here, you are a redneck."

We sat for a minute so she could catch her breath.

"Okay, Jules. I'm not going to beat around the bush. What's going on with you and Sarah Mason?"

"Who?" She choked on her first sip of Miller Lite.

"C'mon. The petite, blue-eyed blonde in the noon linguistics class."

"Nothing, Doc. I swear, I've never even talked to her outside class." She was starting to sweat again.

"Well, you'd have to be blind to miss the chemistry between you two. I haven't ever seen two people have such intense lingering glances. It's starting to make me hot, and that takes a lot."

"Just because two people stare at each other doesn't mean there is something going on. I know better than to ever pursue a student. You made it clear to me when I hit on you that students and faculty do not date."

"Well, you aren't really considered faculty. And I was trying to think of a way to let you down without admitting that I was in a serious relationship. We wouldn't have worked out anyway. We would have argued all the time about pronunciation and poetry perception."

"True. You're in a serious relationship? Do tell."

"You already know about Sam. Don't change the subject. What are you going to do about this sophomore?" I refilled her empty mug.

"I don't know. I get so nervous. I know I'm gay, but I've never . . . you know." She blushed.

"You've never acted on it? But you've been out since high school. You've never been with a woman. Honestly, how do you know you are gay? What if you kiss her and realize that you've made a terrible mistake?" I loved playing the devil's advocate.

"I've been with men, Doc. That was the terrible mistake I made. I figure sex with women has to be better. Worst-case scenario is that I'm asexual and will join a nunnery."

"Don't even joke about the nunnery. Those sisters can be really domineering. I think it's time you made a move. At least ask her out—you don't have to sleep with her. The semester's almost over and you don't know if she will be back in the fall. Besides, the two of you are so distracting that I can't make a coherent statement. The sexual tension is ruining my delightful lectures."

"So I should go after her to make your lectures better. To be honest, they weren't that great to begin with. But in the name of

higher education, I will ask her out. Sheesh, the things I do to as-
sist you in your career." She rolled her eyes to emphasize the sarcasm. "So, I guess you didn't want to talk about the syllabus?"

I smiled my evil smile and poured myself another drink.

We sat in silence for a while and watched the cheesy karaoke
that started in the next room. I racked my brain to come up with
a plan to get them together. Finally, an epiphany: "Hey, I got
that poetry reading thing next week." I tried to make eye contact,
which was impossible for me when I was scheming.

"I know. I will be there, but I'm not reading this time. You
practically booed me off the stage last month."

"Well, Sam's got a dinner thing with her folks. I wasn't going
to go, but I tend to miss too many of her functions. Think you
could cover me and coordinate the reading?"

"I guess so. But you're gonna owe me. One more pitcher and
some nachos."

"Deal." I took my conniving self to the bar, ordered the food
and started planning my next strategy.

Chapter Two

The following Thursday, Jules arrived at the Library, a local bar, twenty minutes before the poetry reading was supposed to begin. She set out some sign-in sheets and ordered herself a cappuccino. Very few students showed up for the event, which relieved her. She didn't mind public speaking, but she feared being heckled in a bar atmosphere. The bar blocked off three hours a month for the reading. Due to the lack of attendance, Jules figured she would be out of there in an hour. She already planned to leave as soon as possible in hopes of making it home in time to see her favorite movie on HBO.

One at a time she introduced the ten readers from the sign-in sheet. Some read quickly and quietly. Others took the stage and made loud, drunken asses of themselves. A few of the people were college students; others were town locals with a penchant for ama-

teur poetry. Either way, everyone had read and left by seven fifteen. Jules waited around another fifteen minutes to see if anyone
else would arrive. She needed to sign in the students so they could
get their extra credit points. No one else showed. On her way out,
she stopped to talk to the bartender and pay for her coffee. As she
turned around, she ran smack dab into a familiar face.

"Sorry, excuse me." Jules blushed as she bent to pick up her
notebook.

"My fault, I wasn't watching my . . . um. My fault." Sarah
blushed back.

"If you're here for the reading, it's pretty much over. It started
at six."

"Oh, Dr. O'Connor gave me this note. It says that the time
was changed and that it started at eight." She handed Jules the
note. "I really wanted to read tonight."

"Ah. A note. Of course." Jules knew what was up. "There will
be another chance to read next month. Doc's not here tonight
anyway and I'm not very good at critiquing."

The two of them stood in awkward silence for what seemed
like hours.

"Jules, here's your change." The bartender broke the silence.

"Keep it, Matt. And start me a tab, please." She turned and
smiled at Sarah. "Care to join me for a drink?"

"She'd better be twenty-one or it's another cappuccino for the
both of you."

"I'm legal, and I would love a screwdriver. Thank you." Sarah
set her poetry book and Texas driver's license on the bar and
pulled up a stool.

Around eight, Sam and I peeked in the window of the bar
to see if my plan had worked. When we saw the two sitting in
silence, sipping mixed drinks, we gave each other a high five and

crept back to the car to head to our imaginary dinner.

Jules smiled at Sarah. "Sorry about the note. I don't know what Doc was thinking."

"No biggie. I thought it was a little strange that she would give me a note anyway. I would have thought she'd make a class announcement."

"Dr. O'Connor works in mysterious ways." Jules rolled her eyes to emphasize the craziness of it all.

"Is it true what they say?" Sarah whispered. "You know, about her being gay?"

"Well, it's not much of a rumor. She's never come out and said anything publicly, but I do have it on good authority that she is dating a woman who used to live right over there." Jules gestured to the house across the street. "I heard they're buying a house in Dallas next year. Must be serious."

"Are you guys pretty good friends?" Sarah stared at Jules's hands.

"We're becoming friends. I met her when I was a freshman, before she was department head. I think she was married to a man back then. I'm not sure." Jules became self-conscious of her hands, wishing she had worn something better than a Mickey Mouse watch. "I like being her assistant, and we hang every once in a while."

"So you guys have never, um," Sarah stammered and sipped her drink.

"Wow, you jump right to the point. No, I've never dated Doc. Why do you assume that I'm gay?"

"I, um. Well, I guess I didn't assume it as much as I hoped you were." She smiled an innocent smile that melted Jules's stomach. "I didn't mean to be so abrupt. I just thought that I should know from the get-go so I don't build you up and walk away crushed."

"So, I take it that you're gay, Sarah?"

"Yup. Sarah Mason, gay and single." She held out her hand.

"Jules Ritchie, also gay and single and at your service." She returned the handshake.

Classes were pretty much back to normal after their encounter. Jules seemed able to concentrate with very few lingering glances in Sarah's direction. I took personal pleasure in the fact that I brought the two innocent lambs together. I hoped the lack of flirtation meant they had established a connection, not that they hated each other. I made it my personal goal to pry immediately.

"Sam's in town this week. Care to join us for lunch?" I asked the following Wednesday as I handed her my roll sheet.

"Okay, but you're buyin'."

"How come you say that every time I ask you to do anything?"

"I'm a starving student. You're the one that makes a fortune." She laughed.

"I'm the one who should be laughing. If you think teachers make a lot of money, then you'd better change your major, chickee. I think Sam can afford to buy us both lunch."

"Oh, yeah, what does she do?"

I didn't have the heart to tell her that not only was I in love with a beautiful femme, but that my femme was from a wealthy family. "She works at a hotel and she's in school." Okay, it was law school and she owned the hotel. Same difference.

"She's a starving student too? I'll order light."

We arrived at the crowded Maple Street Café and Sam was holding a table. The three of us ordered chef's salads and made small talk. I was surprised at how much Jules and Sam had in common—they were immediately admiring each other's clothing style. I almost regretted making the introduction, so I veered the conversation to talk of Sarah.

"How did the reading go this week?"

"It was fine. No one really showed up." She was going to play it evasive.

"Is that right?" I loved a challenge. "Anything interesting happen?"

"Dani, give her a break." Sam knew what nosy game I was playing.

"Dani? That's right! Your name is Dani." Jules laughed at me.

"Sorry, Doc, I forgot where we were."

"Well, as if you didn't know, Dr. Dani, Sarah showed up two hours late and showed me your little note." Her tone was playful. "We sat at the bar until midnight and got a little tipsy."

"Is she even old enough to drink?" My conservative side always comes out when I discuss my students.

"Just barely. She's pretty cool. Yes, she is gay, as I am sure you were well aware, given your expertise in the matter." She nodded at Sam.

As we sat and sipped iced tea, Jules told us all about their conversation. She gave me some major insight into Sarah's past and her own. I learned a lot about Jules and knew I didn't need to worry about her getting a crush on my Sam. After one simple meeting, Jules was way past smitten with Sarah.

"So what's next on the agenda. Gonna ask her to go out Friday?" Sam was being the nosy one now.

"Oh, gosh, no. We've only talked once. I couldn't possibly ask her out." Jules seemed uneasy suddenly and began twirling her hair.

Sam and I exchanged an incredulous glance and laughed at the obvious.

I said, "Lady, how do you expect to talk to her if you don't try to spend time with her?"

"I don't know. I didn't really think about that. Maybe you could meddle again and make some magic happen." She held up her hand to show her crossed fingers.

"I think I've done enough. My plate is pretty full right now." I glanced at Sam, looking for some help out of the predicament.

"Jules, honestly, I'm amazed that Doc has become so interested in your love life. She never interferes with her students." Sam knew better than to tell Jules about my sister being on her deathbed and my dealing with the recent announcement of my ex-husband and his new wife getting pregnant. "I think we can help her out one more time though." She winked my direction.

"Really, that would be great." Jules was grinning from ear to ear.

"I'm heading back to California on Monday. It would have to be this weekend." Sam's wheels were evidently turning.

"That's fine. I can make myself available."

"Sam, I need to be careful. Sarah is a student, and although there are rumors about me, I'm really not ready to be fully outed in front of the whole university." My conservative nature got the best of me once again.

"Doc, she pretty much knows you're gay. C'mon. If you do this for me, I'll grade all the final exams and even fill out my own evaluation."

"Wow, fill out your own evaluation. That's mighty big of you." Actually, I did hate evaluating my assistants.

"Dani, um, Doc and I are going to Shreveport for the weekend." Sam beamed.

"We are?" I wasn't prepared for a weekend of gluttony.

"Yes, we are. You're welcome to come along and bring Sarah. You guys can drive out with us and I'll get you each your own room."

"I think that's a bit much for a first date. I couldn't afford it anyway."

I gave my evil look to Sam, meaning, please don't start the "it's on us" speech. I knew she could afford it, but I didn't want the awkwardness of explaining, and I really didn't want to spend four hours in a car with college kids. Thankfully she let me off the hook.

"Okay, I guess that is a bit much for a first date. How about we save Shreveport for another time. Let's do the gayville thing. You two can meet us in Dallas on Friday night and we can hit the strip." It seemed her wheels were turning slower.

"That sounds pretty good to me. Think she'll go for it? I don't even know if she likes gay bars." The insecurity of youth was in Jules as she spoke. I remembered that feeling of wonder from when I was her age.

"She'll go for it," Sam and I said in unison, knowing that no woman could say no to this vibrant teaching assistant.

Chapter Three

Jules decided to skip her last two classes on Friday. She took off early and went to the gym, the bank and the mall. The last three hundred dollars was pulled from her checking account and half of that was put toward a new pair of sandals, faded jeans and a crisp white shirt. She counted the other hundred and fifty over and over again with much scrutiny. She couldn't believe she was taking that much money on a date. She couldn't believe that she actually had a date. It had taken her four months to earn that extra three hundred dollars and she'd meant to put it in savings for a plane ticket home to her family. The fact that she was using the money on Sarah confirmed her suspicion that she had really met someone special.

She stood in front of the mirror for twenty minutes debating her hairstyle. She knew she should have had it cut, but that would have dipped into her date money. She hoped that it would be windy in Dallas so she didn't have to apologize for her ratty hair. She loved her new shirt and reveled in the fact that she finally had a reason to spend money on that dreamy French-cuffed classic. The jeans fit great, but the sandals were a bit of a problem. They looked perfect with her clothes and freshly painted toenails. The problem was that they made a sort of "farting" noise on about every third step. She paced up and down the hall of her small apartment for half an hour in hopes that the incriminating noise would go away. No luck. She had her heart set on wearing her new shoes, though, and vowed that even a little gassy accusation wouldn't stop her.

Finally, after checking and rechecking her makeup, she was ready for her first real date with a woman. She went over her list to make sure she had everything she needed. She even brought a pack of cigarettes in case Sarah smoked. Jules recounted her money one last time and decided to put a twenty back in the drawer in case they made lunch plans for the next day. She had never gone to gay bars before and prayed that a hundred and thirty would be enough for an evening in the city.

Sarah missed all of her classes on Friday due to a nasty hangover. She had gone out Thursday night with her sister, gotten tipsy and confessed the fact that she was a lesbian. Her sister was thrilled that Sarah was happy and insisted on celebrating into the wee hours of Friday. Sarah didn't have the heart to tell her that she wanted to be fresh and alert for her first date on Friday, so she drank every single Colorado Bulldog that her sister placed in front of her. Sarah slept until two, woke up and cursed at the mess in the kitchen and then went to McDonald's.

After choking down two Happy Meals, she attempted a cigarette. The nicotine went straight to her head and her stomach; an hour in the bathroom followed. She debated canceling the date with Jules but refused, knowing that she may never get another chance with such a beautiful woman, her fantasy woman. By four o'clock, she was feeling a little better and managed to pull together a shower.

She heard her sister come in and immediately cursed her name. "Damn it, Melinda! I'm hung over as a bitch and I missed all my classes today!"

Melinda popped her head into the bathroom and laughed at the sight of her green sister standing under the cold water of the shower. "I'm sorry, love. I just wanted your outing to be memorable. Go back to bed. It's the weekend!"

"I can't. I have a date and she's picking me up in two hours."

"Oh, shit. You should have told me that last night. Wait here. I'll be right back."

Melinda returned from the kitchen with a six-pack of Shiner Bock and some aspirin.

"Take three of these, and three of these, and you will be fine in a jiff."

"Great, then I'll be drunk before she even gets here."

"Nah, it's a college fact that beer gets rid of hangovers and you can't get as drunk as fast the second night."

Sarah thought about it, and although it didn't seem right, she trusted her sister's knowledge of alcohol. Melinda had been a bartender for several years. "This better work or I'll kill you." She choked down the aspirin with some beer. "I'm just glad Mom and Dad aren't here to see this," she said as vomit entered her throat.

"Me too. They'd shit if they knew you had a date with a woman. Where are you going tonight anyway?" Melinda opened a beer of her own.

"She called it gayville? Some area of downtown Dallas?"

"Oh, cool! You can disco all night long. Have you ever danced with a woman?"

"I've never even been to a gay bar, Melinda. Dancing and all other contact is new to me as well. I just hope this beer stays down and my hair stays up."

"I'm off to work. Good luck."

Sarah took a few moments to press her favorite black shirt, the one with the French cuffs. She went back and forth for a bit on the jeans: with holes or without? She chose the trendier jeans with holes in the knees and butt then slipped into her favorite black boots. She sprayed her hair again and again to the point that it was stiff enough to stand forever. She finished two of the three suggested beers and took two more aspirin. She emptied her wallet of its cash, ID and credit cards, then grabbed a lighter and a fresh pack of cigarettes. After checking her hair and makeup three more times, she was ready for her big night on the town.

"Sam, we have to meet them in twenty minutes. Are you gonna get dressed?"

"Yeah." Sam pulled herself away from the computer and strolled toward the closet.

"What are you wearing tonight?" I was still lounging on the bed at Sam's hotel.

"I dunno. I'll just throw on some jeans and an oxford. What are you wearing?"

"Same old, same old. Jeans and snap-buttoned shirt. Got any cash?"

"A little, I'll run a tab and use a card. Got any smokes?"

"Yeah." I pulled a wrinkled soft pack from my cargo shorts, then I threw on my clothes, brushed my teeth. We were out the door a few minutes later.

The sound of the doorbell startled Sarah and suddenly she felt sick to her stomach again. She stood still until the nausea subsided then opened the squeaky oak door.

An awkward moment seemed to last ten minutes before Jules finally spoke. "Hi. You look really nice. Are you ready to go?"

"You look nice too. Want to come in?" She immediately regretted asking once she remembered the condition of the kitchen.

"No, thanks. We need to get on the road if we want to meet Doc and Sam on time."

Sarah shrugged and stepped onto the porch. After locking the door, she followed Jules to her beat-up truck. Halfway down the sidewalk, Sarah swore she heard an odd noise coming from Jules' direction. She tried really hard not to laugh.

"New shoes," Jules said and laughed, not sure if Sarah bought it.

They sat in silence most of the way to Dallas. Sarah was nervous, not quite knowing where to start.

Finally, thirty minutes into the drive and ten miles from their destination she broke the ice. "That's really cool that Dr. O'Connor and her girlfriend invited us out with them."

"Yeah. She made a point of asking us to keep it hush-hush on campus."

"That's no problem. If I out her, then I out myself." Sarah realized that she just admitted the fact that she remained closeted.

"Yeah, me too."

"Why are we meeting them at a hotel?"

"I think Sam works there and they stay there on the weekends. Seems pretty cool that they get a free room."

"What does she do for the hotel?"

"I'm not sure, maybe a desk clerk or somethin'."

Jules had done as she was told and left her truck with the valet. She and Sarah entered the hotel lobby and frantically looked around for us. Sam and I lingered in the corner just inside the lounge and observed their awkwardness. They were standing five feet apart and they both had their hands in their pockets.

"Oh, boy. This should be fun," I whispered and began to stand.

"Well, I think I see a lot of alcohol in our future. Maybe in their future too. Are you sure she's twenty-one? She doesn't look a day over fifteen." Sam sucked the last drop from her Corona bottle.

"Yeah, I double-checked. I didn't want to get fired for contributing to the delinquency of a minor."

We motioned for them to join us. They kept their same five-foot distance on the walk over. I introduced Sam to Sarah, but the conversation died. The two youngsters didn't make eye contact with each other, and I could tell Sam was instantly annoyed with the tension in our group.

"Do you want to stay here for a bit, or are you ready to head out?" I was hoping they wanted to leave, fearing someone might blow Sam's cover.

"We could stay here for a bit." They actually spoke in unison, so maybe there was hope for them yet.

Sam signaled the lounge waitress and ordered a bottle of champagne. Jules and Sarah seemed impressed, but I could tell they felt awkward. I was relieved that we were brought a bottle of Moët and not Dom. I didn't want to overwhelm the girls on their first outing.

"I've never really had champagne." Sarah held her glass to the light.

"I had it once at a wedding. I'm more of a beer drinker, myself," Jules added.

Sam was probably ready to scream. I fully expected her to make some pretentious remark, although she didn't have a pretentious bone in her body. She just lacked patience. "Well, you always remember the first time you drink champagne. That is, unless you drink too much."

Finally, some small talk ensued, and everyone began to loosen up. I tried not to talk about school, but the conversation kept veering that way. I asked the girls about their families and life outside the university. They responded with one-word answers, as if they were interviewing for a job they didn't really want. I had no idea what to do to break the ice. I could tell that Sam's wheels were turning, and I hoped it didn't involve tequila shooters and a stripper.

"Hey, Doc, tell them about the time you had diarrhea on the flight to London."

I shot Sam a "fuck you" smile and blushed. "Well, dear, why don't you tell them about the time you fell off the cruise ship."

She returned the "fuck you" smile, and I knew it was war. "Remember the time you dated a transsexual?"

"Remember the time you thought you kissed your cousin?"

"Aren't you the English professor who failed her freshman grammar midterm?"

"Aren't you the law student who didn't know who Clarence Darrow was?" I shot back.

"Show them the tattoo on your shoulder and your naval ring, sweetie."

"Show them your hemorrhoid, honeybunch." I couldn't help but to burst out laughing on that one. Sam couldn't help it either. We both fell into a fit of laughter. Jules and Sarah stared at us like we were crazy. They had that look of a deer caught in the headlights, and it was priceless. Sam and I took one long look at them and laughed even harder.

Jules said, "Wow, you two really seem to know each other."

"More like how to push each other's buttons." I winked at Sam.

"How did you meet?" Jules sipped her champagne.

It was the question I always dreaded. We had our initial contact through a dating site, but technically, we talked at a pool hall months before the Net meeting.

"We are figments of each other's imagination." Sam gave her pat answer.

I gave mine. "It's like we're imaginary friends with benefits."

"Dr. O'Connor, what was y'alls first date like?" Sarah nervously forced out the question.

"Well, our first date was the evening after the first time we really met. We were both terribly nervous and shy and not much really happened." I had to giggle.

Sam decided to step in with the truth. "We came downtown, much like you guys did tonight. We got shitty drunk and Dr. O'Connor spent the night with me in the hotel." She had a wicked sparkle in her eye. "Of course nothing happened. I just didn't want her to drink and drive."

"Okay, I think it's time to hit the strip. We can probably walk from here. It's a nice night." I didn't want the details of our private life to go any further with my students. Jules and Sarah stood and both reached into their pockets for money.

"The champagne is already taken care of. You guys can get it next time." Sam signed a bogus receipt and left a ten for a tip. "It's kind of sexy the way she calls you Dr. O'Connor," Sam whispered as we exited the lobby. "But why don't you tell her to call you Doc?"

"I don't know. It's kind of fun to just make her squirm. I have a feeling that neither of these two has even kissed a woman. Part of me wants to give them the best night of their lives, and the other part of me wants to ground them for being boring and send them to their rooms."

"Yeah, I know what you mean. Let's just make it fun for them. Drop the tired professor routine and let's show them what it's like being gay in this wonderful town."

"Deal, but Jules had better quit farting when she walks. It's freakin' me out."

Chapter Four

I would imagine that anyone would look terrified the first time they stepped foot in a gay-boy country bar. The reality of all those pretty men doing the two-step is enough to make any gay person run back to the shelter of their closet, especially a newbie. It probably didn't help that the little corner of the bar we sat down in was having some sort of drag queen convention. If I didn't know better, I would have sworn that I saw my Great-Aunt Mildred, but it was just a large hairy guy in a pink polyester halter top.

It was obvious that Jules was trying hard not to stare. She kept looking at the guys and turning her head really fast if they glanced her way. Sarah was doing a little better; she kept her eyes on the floor and only glanced up when someone spoke. Sam returned from the bar with four beers and a cup of popcorn.

"You shouldn't eat that," Jules said the minute the greasy cup was set on the table.

"Yeah, there are major germs in community bar food," Sarah added.

"What's the matter, afraid homosexuality is catching?" Sam laughed.

"No, I just read that only six percent of men wash their hands in the bathroom."

"Really?" Jules murmured, "I heard it was twelve percent."

At least the two were talking.

Sam reached her hand into the cup and forced a fistful of popcorn into her mouth. The girls both cringed. "Get over it, ladies. These are gay boys. They all wash their hands in the bathroom. It's what they touch on the dance floor that you need to worry about."

The repulsion of bar food actually sparked a long conversation between the two daters. They went on and on, back and forth for thirty minutes about all their quirks. Who knew two people could have so much OCD in common? Apparently you shouldn't set your purse on the table, or your luggage on the bed. These things have touched airport bathroom floors, you know. And you should never, ever let your pillow hit the floor. You see, your shoes walk on the floor—the same shoes that walk in public restrooms. Don't even get them started about holding dirty menus or borrowing a pen at a gas station to sign your credit card receipt. If they ever decided to live together, I thought, it would be in a very sterile home with no pillows.

I was surprised to see that Sarah smoked. I don't know why I assumed she didn't; maybe it was the pure and innocent student image I had of her. I resisted the temptation to tell her that she shouldn't smoke because cigarettes contained rat parts, and rats walk on bathroom floors. I pulled the wrinkled pack of Marlboros from my pocket and asked her for a light.

"I didn't know you smoked, Dr. O'Connor." Sarah leaned in to light my cigarette.

"There are lots of things you don't know about me, Sarah." I smiled. "And you can call me Doc."

"Is Doc your real name?"

"No, it's my initials. But I worked really hard to get my degree so it would make sense."

"What's your real name?" The beer had loosened her up.

"I would tell you, but then I'd have to fail you." I hated my real first name.

"So it starts with a D. If I guess it, will you tell me?"

"If you guess it, your grade will start with a D." I loved the power of the student-teacher relationship.

Sam finally persuaded Jules to try a little two-step. I took the opportunity to interrogate Sarah. "Want to play a little game of twenty drinking questions?"

"That's a new one. How do I play?" She smiled.

"It's easy. I ask you a question, and you answer. If you don't want to answer, you take a sip of beer. If you do answer, you ask me a question. If you take the beer shot, I ask another. Got it?"

"Yes, but I should warn you, I can drink a lot of beer." She held up her bottle.

I went to the bar and got us four more beers and gave Sam the signal that they should stay on the dance floor for a while longer. Sam rolled her eyes and pointed at her feet. Apparently Jules was a worse dancer than I. Maybe Jules was farting while she danced.

"Okay, Sarah. Where did you grow up?"

"San Antonio. What's your first name?" You could tell she was dying to know.

I took a very long sip of beer.

"Okay. I get to ask another. Do you have a brother or sister, Doc?"

"Yes, both. Do you have siblings?"

"Yes, a sister named Melinda. I just came out to her last night. Does your family know you're gay, Doc?"

I took another sip of beer.

Sarah chuckled. "I ask again. Are you in love with Sam?"

"Since the moment I kissed her neck. Have you ever had a girlfriend?"

"No. But I was engaged to a guy last year. What's it like to sleep with a woman?"

"Worth the wait. Be patient. How much wood could a woodchuck chuck if a woodchuck could chuck wood?" I didn't want to discuss the topic of sex with a sophomore, even if she was twenty-one.

"About two forests. Depends on the size of the woodchuck. Were you really married to a man?"

I took a very long sip of beer. Fortunately, Sam and Jules returned from the dance floor.

"Hey, we were just playing twenty questions." I batted my eyelashes, indicating how truly bored I was.

"Oh, did Doc ask the woodchuck question?" Sam knew I would ask that if the question of sex came up."

"Yeah. I said two forests."

"The answer is two-point-eight cords of wood. Two even if they're solid oak."

No one could tell if Sam was serious. Even I had to think about that oak thing.

"You got a better question that doesn't involve a woodchuck?" I was ready for a good intellectual debate and could count on Sam to give us one.

"Actually, there is something I've wanted to discuss with you." Sam looked serious.

"You want us to leave you guys for a bit?" Jules seemed worried.

"No, I think I need some backup. I know Doc is no doubt going to take the opposing side on this one."

I took a long sip of my beer. "Okay, Sam. Shoot." I was ready for battle and knew something extremely goofy was fixin' to fall from my girl's mouth.

"Who would win in a wrestling match between Dixie Carter and Judith Light?"

"That depends. Is it WWF wrestling or is there mud involved?" Jules asked without missing a beat.

"They're wrestling in a vat of Jell-O, it's televised and there are no rules."

"Is it televised on ESPN or Lifetime?" Sarah chimed in.

"What difference will that make?" I was impressed with their willingness to participate.

"Well, if it's on Lifetime, Judith will have the advantage because of the hundreds of movies she's made for that channel. The referees would give her a bit of leeway."

Sam nodded. "Good point. It's on HBO, live from Vegas. Neither has the home court advantage."

"It should be obvious that Dixie would kick Judith's ass." I was certain this would be the outcome.

"I knew you would say that, Doc. Give us two reasons." Sam challenged me.

"Well, first of all, 'Dixie' is a pretty tough name. Anyone could beat up a 'Judith,' but it takes a really strong broad to wrestle a 'Dixie' to the floor."

"That's true. But Judith plays some strong characters. In her movies, she's been in prison, tried to kill her daughter, killed a bunch of husbands and I think she was even a serial arsonist." Sarah was getting into the debate.

"No, she wasn't a serial arsonist; she just burned down one house. But those are good points. Dixie has only played an interior designer. Anyone could wrestle a designer." Jules smiled.

"Careful. Don't talk about interior designers too loudly in this bar." Sam laughed. "Okay, Doc. Two more reasons."

"Well, Dixie is stinky. She could make someone fall to the ground based on smell alone."

"Stinky? What the hell does that mean?" Sam raised an eyebrow.

"Sometimes when you look at people on TV, don't you sometimes wonder what they smell like? See, Gregory Peck probably smelled wonderful, like aftershave. But to me, Dixie Carter is queen of the stink."

"I wouldn't talk about queens in this bar either. What does Dixie stink like?" Jules seemed intrigued.

"This is just a guess. I could be wrong, but I think she smells like dirty pantyhose and stale cigarettes." I thought for a moment. "And occasionally steamed cabbage."

"Cabbage? You never mentioned cabbage before." Sam laughed.

"Well, she is getting older. I would imagine that she is eating softer foods. Older people love cooked cabbage, don't they?" I took another long sip of beer. "Of course, Judith has more staying power. Over the past ninety-six years she has made no fewer than two million Lifetime movies." I waited for the joke to sink in. "In all that time, she looks the same, and actually she seems to get more wiry with age. So while Dixie is filtering cabbage through unwashed pantyhose while chain-smoking. Judith is constantly on the set, training for her next prison scene."

"*Ding ding*. I think we have a winner here. Judith beats Dixie." Sam held up my hand like the match was over.

"I'm gonna have to argue." Sarah was on the edge of her chair. "I think Dixie has the advantage by being out of show business."

"Wait, isn't Dixie Carter dead?" Jules looked confused.

"No, just her career." Sarah continued, "It is possible that

Dixie has been at home training for this match for the last ten years. Judith is filming nine movies a week and may not have time to train. What if Dixie keeps her pool filled with gelatin and works out three times a day?"

"Ooh, good point." Jules added, "We don't know what she's done since her career died. I think at Judith's house, every time the phone rings she can assume it's a Lifetime director calling her in for another role. I would imagine that Dixie doesn't need to waste her energy answering phones. That right there is saved up energy that she can use in the ring."

"Hmm. After weighing both sides, I believe we may have a tie. Judith is more wiry and still active. But we don't know Dixie's training regimen for the last ten years. I believe it's a tossup." Sam seemed disappointed. I think she really wanted Judith to win.

Everyone's spirit was high and the conversation was really rolling. The Judith/Dixie debate really proved that these girls not only had a sense of humor but also a lot in common. I started to feel comfortable with both of them and hoped they would hook up so we could double-date again. We walked across the street to one of the lesbian bars and immediately found a table near the dance floor. Sam and I switched to drinking water, knowing that we had a lot to do on Saturday. Jules and Sarah both kept on drinking beer, which made me glad that we had reserved extra rooms at the hotel.

Sam and Sarah went to wait in the long bathroom lines which left me a chance to play twenty questions with Jules.

"So, how's it going for you?" I shouted over the loud dance music.

"I'm having fun. I didn't realize there were so many gay people in this city."

"Well, this is hardly all of them. It's not like they all come to the bars every Friday night. I'd say you could safely bet that there are at least twenty-three more gay people who couldn't make it out tonight." I had to laugh at my own joke.

"I want to ask Sarah to dance, but Sam told me I was a lousy dancer."

"Well, country dancing is a lot harder than dancing to Cher. Just shift your weight and move your hips. Try not to go too crazy with the arms and hand gestures. The good news is that they don't play anything slow in here. So it's not like a junior high dance where you go from 'Rock Lobster' to an Air Supply song."

"Who's Air Supply? What's 'Rock Lobster'?"

"Oh, my dear child. Bless your little heart." I suddenly felt ancient. "Just do what comes naturally with Sarah. You don't have to do anything but have fun. My guess is that she's just as scared about being around women as you are."

"Did she tell you that?" Jules seemed relieved.

"No, but you can see it on her face. Poor girl looks terrified. She did try to take your hand when we walked over here. You missed that one. But at least she made the first move."

Jules beamed with the newfound confidence she needed, and the minute Sam and Sarah returned from the bathroom, Jules escorted her to the dance floor. Sarah didn't really reach for Jules' hand, but I loved being the instigator.

"Dani, we need to get going." Sam looked upset, and she rarely called me Dani.

"Okay, do you feel all right?" Her concerned look worried me.

"I'm fine. Listen, Jack left a message at the hotel and they paged me. Amy's in pretty bad shape. You need to get down to Houston."

They were words I was dreading and they sounded so much worse when Sam had to shout them over the loud music. She was gone to the bathroom for ten minutes. How could so much have changed in ten minutes? Immediately I hated her for carrying a pager and cell phone. I hated myself for being out having a good time. Moreover, I hated the world for giving cancer to my twin sister.

"We should tell them we're leaving." I motioned toward the dance floor.

"No, I already talked to Sarah. I gave her the room keys and told her to take a cab back to the hotel. She's going to tell Jules that you won't be teaching this week and that she should take over your classes until further notice."

"Wow, you did all that in ten minutes?" I didn't know what else to say.

"Well, I . . . yeah, baby." You could tell she almost made a joke and knew better.

We motioned to the dancing partners and headed toward the door. Jules looked concerned. I guessed that Sarah hadn't told her yet. The cab ride back to the hotel seemed to take forever.

"Where are they going?" Jules leaned toward Sarah's ear and had the urge to kiss her.

"What?" Sarah shouted back over the music, then led Jules off the dance floor.

"Where are they going?" Jules asked again when they got to the quiet beer garden in the back of the bar.

"Doc's sister is sick. Sam got a page and called someone on her cell when we were in the bathroom."

"Oh, I didn't know she even had a sister."

"She does, actually. They're twins. Danielle and Amy. Dani."

"Sam told you Doc's name? It must be something serious." Jules leaned on the bar.

"It's pretty bad, Jules. She has ovarian cancer. Sam said you need to take over classes until further notice."

"Man, that sucks."

"Sucks that you have to teach this week?"

"No, it sucks to think that someone could lose her twin sister. Do you want to head for home?" Jules didn't feel like dancing anymore.

"Actually, Sam gave me these." She held up two room keys. "She told us to take a cab back to the hotel and to feel free to stay. Your truck is there anyway."

"Oh." Jules didn't want to admit it but said, "I don't think I have enough cash with me to pay for a hotel room."

"Well, I got the impression that we didn't have to pay. She even gave me ten bucks for a cab. But I might be able to cover half a room. We could turn in one key and share a room in case we do get charged." Sarah blushed a deep crimson.

"Yeah, I could probably cover half. We could walk back and use that extra ten bucks for a drink in the lobby bar. Sound good?"

"Well, Sam said she wasn't comfortable with us walking alone around here since we didn't know the area. But I'm always up for an adventure. I'm not worried if you're not."

"Nah. I think an adventure with you sounds fun. I feel pretty safe when you're around anyway." Jules leaned closer to Sarah. She started to kiss her but then just reached for her hand instead.

"You are safe with me." Sarah stood on her tiptoes and kissed Jules' neck.

A half-hour later they were standing in the hotel lobby.

"What is the going rate for a room here?" Sarah asked the lady at the front desk who told her they started at $150 and went up to $725.

"But we don't have any vacancies tonight."

"We already have two rooms, but we only need one." Sarah reddened. "Can we turn in one key and keep the cheaper room?"

The desk clerk took the keys. "Well, they are both smoking

suites. The rate is six-fifty for one and four-fifty for the other."
She looked at the computer screen and smiled.

"Oh, well, we should probably turn in both keys then." Jules
was disappointed.

"Actually, these rooms are taken care of. Room service charges, bar charges and brunch are included as well." She handed the
keys back to Sarah. "Do you still want to cancel one room?"

"Um, well, I don't know." Jules looked at Sarah, who grinned
and took the lead.

"Yes, please. Cancel the more expensive room. How late is the
bar open?"

"The bar is open until two. Are you sure you want to cancel
the larger room? I know that Miss Laine won't mind either way.
It's doubtful anyone else will come in for a suite at this hour."

"Miss Laine? You mean Sam?"

"Yes, Samantha Laine, the hotel's owner."

"We'll take the smaller room, but we'll run up the bar tab."
Sarah laughed, grabbed the key and led Jules to the bar.

Chapter Five

I called my brother Jack the minute we got to the room.

"They're saying it could be a week, maybe two at the most." He sounded exhausted.

"Is she coherent?"

"She is. She's just very weak. I think she's in a lot of pain. Her friends got here this morning, but they're leaving on Tuesday."

"What about Mom and Dad?"

"Mom gets in Sunday. Dad has to close up the factory and will fly in on Wednesday."

"Why is he closing the factory?" The others could run it, I thought.

"He said he didn't want any distractions. He wants to focus on Amy."

"What are your plans?" I tried not to think of my parents.

"I'll head back to Dallas after Mom gets here Sunday. I have appointments that I need to keep. I'll probably work until Wednesday then cancel patients as long as I need to. I'll be back in Houston on Thursday."

"Why didn't you call me sooner, Jack?" I started to cry.

"Doc, it happened really fast. She seemed fine yesterday. They even thought she could go home next week. Just since this morning she has declined fifty percent."

"Maybe we should bring her home. Maybe she would rather . . ." I couldn't even say it.

"No. It's too late to move her. She is better off here." His voice broke.

"I can drive down tonight." I tried to sound prepared.

"No. Let her have tomorrow with her friends, and a day with Mom. Come down Monday night and she can have you to herself on Tuesday before Dad arrives."

"What if—" I couldn't continue.

"Dani, I promise there's enough time. Wait till Monday. Let Mom have a day with her alone."

"Can I do anything?" I felt so helpless.

"Go by my house and get the photo album. There's also a box above the washer marked 'Twins.' Grab it too. Bring some of your pajamas. Hers are too big now. She likes your cowboy pajamas—" He started crying really hard and the phone went dead.

I continued to hold the receiver to my ear and listened to the dial tone. I could feel Sam coming up behind me and I didn't move. I stared out the window and watched the valets and bellhops greeting guests. How nice, I thought, it would be to be a guest tonight and not have a care in the world. How nice it would be to be staying at the beautiful Laine Hotel while vacationing in Dallas. How nice it would be to be anywhere else, instead of lost in my own little world, a world I came into with Amy by my side, a world in which I would be by her side when she died.

"Doc, tell me what I can do." Sam had obviously been crying.

"Nothing, there's nothing you can do." My response sounded bitter, even to my own ears. I swallowed my tears, and the hard lump in my throat made my voice sound shaky. I tried to think about what I could do to get through the next few days before I left for Houston. All I could think about was getting drunk and sleeping a lot. "Let's go downstairs."

"I don't think alcohol is the answer, baby. Don't you need to pack?"

"I'm going down on Monday. My mom will be there, and her friends are there. Jack thinks Amy needs some time with them alone." The numbness was setting in and my tears retreated. I felt angry, and I didn't need someone telling me what the answer was. "Please, let's just go downstairs."

"Doc, we have beer up here. Let's just stay in the room and talk."

"I don't want to talk, dreamer. I want to be around the hotel guests. I want to sit in the bar with happy people who are on vacation. I want to feel a sense of normalcy. I want to postpone my thoughts for one more day. I want to go sit in the fucking bar!"

Sam looked stunned by my reaction. I'm sure the look on my face scared the shit out of her. "Okay, baby. Let's go downstairs." She slipped on her shoes and handed me mine. I stared at them, unsure of what I was supposed to do with them. The thought of shoes suddenly seemed foreign to me. Sam got on her knees and slipped the sandals onto my feet. "No shirt, no shoes, no service. It's a strict policy in this hotel."

"Hey, look who just came in. Maybe everything's okay." Sarah gestured toward the door.

"Should we wave? Maybe we should leave them alone. They

look pretty worn out."

"Let's just sit here. If they want to talk, they'll come over here." Sarah seemed to have an answer for all the etiquette dilemmas, for which Jules was grateful.

"Anyway, what were we talking about? Oh, yeah. I had a Datsun when I was in high school. One night when I was at a football game, it got stolen. I think the stereo was actually worth more than the car itself." Jules chuckled.

"You think someone stole the entire car to get your stereo?"

"It was probably easier. So after that, I had to go without a car until college. I bought my truck about two years ago. It's a piece of junk, but it's paid for and it runs pretty good. What about you?"

"I got my first car when I was seventeen. My dad called one afternoon and said he'd bought me a car. I was so excited. I asked him what kind it was and I thought he said Mazda. When he got home that evening, I went running outside and found a brown and gold 'seventy-seven Monza."

"What on earth is a Monza?"

"It was a Chevy. They only made them in the Seventies and early Eighties. This one had a spider painted on the hood. Mine was so worn out that I had duct tape holding the seats together. I had to use the passenger seat belt to hold the door closed. I was so pissed at my dad that I didn't speak to him for weeks."

"I bet he didn't understand why you were mad."

"Yeah, he did the whole 'I bought you a car, what more do you want?' speech. When I graduated high school, he redeemed himself. He was making a little more money and really did get me a Mazda. I loaned it to my sister a year ago and she swears the telephone pole jumped in front of her. Now I have to work on forgiving her."

"Did she total it?" Jules took a cigarette from Sarah's pack.

"No, but there's a nasty dent on the front end. I used the

insurance money to buy books last semester. I think about getting it fixed, but I'd rather wait and just buy a new car. I've been saving up."

"You work at Crazy Ozzies?"

"Yeah, my sister, Melinda, is a bartender there. I wait tables a few nights a week and I do their advertising." Sarah lit Jules's cigarette. "I didn't know you smoked."

"I'm up for trying new things tonight." She smiled.

"Really, I'll have to keep that in mind." Sarah laughed.

"So. You do all the advertising. Are you the one responsible for writing those awful radio ads?"

"Not only do I write them, but that's me on the radio. I'm a communications major. I hope to go into radio or television when I graduate. If I graduate, that is."

"If?" Jules feared that her new friend might be leaving.

"I was already offered a job. It's a really good offer, great money and benefits."

"Will you be moving?" Jules tried to sound casual.

"No, it's with a cable channel in Fort Worth. My sister doesn't charge me rent, so I figured I'd make that hour-long commute for a year or two."

"If you take the job, you mean."

"I'm pretty sure I'm gonna take it."

"Well, don't let Dr. O'Connor hear you say that. She'd be really upset to see you drop out of school. She said you have a great future," Jules lied.

Sam glanced around the bar. "The girls are sitting over there. Do you want to join them?"

"Maybe in a minute. I'd like to see the end of the game." With a shot glass clenched in my fist, I stared at the small TV behind the bar. I didn't even know who was playing, but I think we were winning. Out of the corner of my eye, I could see Sam waving in the direction of the coeds.

"Mark, send a fruit and cheese plate to table seventeen. Add it to my tab."

"Yes, Miss Laine. Anything for you?"

Sam looked at me and I shrugged. I didn't care if I ever ate again. "Ms. O'Connor will have another shot of tequila and another beer. I'll take a beer and some nuts."

"Send a bowl of mixed nuts to table seventeen, Mark," I said with a smile.

"Oh, that's hysterical. Yes, take them a bowl of nuts before you serve the cheese."

"Take them a block of cheese, and maybe Jules will cut it." I smiled again and Sam started giggling.

"A block of cheese, Miss Laine?" Mark was out of the loop.

"No, the regular tray of slices. Thanks." She turned toward me. "You're pretty funny sometimes."

"Not bad for a woman who is fixin' to lose half her identity." I couldn't believe I said that.

"Well, Doc, I have no idea how to respond to that. You are very funny, nonetheless."

I was almost to the point of being giddy. I didn't feel like crying as much as I really wanted to laugh. I was the type of person who always made light in a crisis. I usually got the giggles at funerals. I figured I would outgrow it, but I think it's just how I am. I really wanted to laugh out loud. I feared what Sam would think if I did. Would she think I was callous, or would she leave me for someone who was more serious? I was trying so hard to fight the tears that the laughter broke through. I stared at the TV screen and giggled.

"What's up, Doc?" She giggled along with me. The phrasing of the question made me laugh harder.

"Do you think Sarah has noticed Jules's farting yet?" I was on a roll.

"Oh. How could she not? Thank heavens that the bars are loud. Good thing we got them separate rooms. I think Jules has a poo on deck."

"What?!" I was laughing so hard, I spilled my beer.

"You know. A poo on deck. I believe when someone farts more than five times that they have to take a dump."

"Wow, that's a very eloquent theory. You don't think it's possible for someone to just have a bit of gas?"

"No. I think four farts means that it's gas. Anything more than four is a definite indication that a movement is forthcoming," she said through titters.

"Oh, that's bad." I took a deep breath. "Is it bad that I have the giggles? I should be up in the room crying my eyes out."

"No, emotion is emotion. People laugh when they're nervous. I would imagine that you have a billion different things in your head. If you need to release, and laughter works, then I say laugh." She gripped my arm.

"You won't think I'm heartless and leave me?"

"I'm here for the duration, and you are anything but heartless."

We sat and made jokes and laughed so loud that I thought the bartender was going to ask us to leave. Just when I thought I was starting to calm down, a cashew flew from the other side of the bar and hit Sam square on the forehead. The snickering started all over again. I nearly peed.

"So, you just came out to Melinda last night?" Jules asked.

"Uh-huh." Sarah sipped her drink. "She was oddly happy. I think it explained a lot of why I didn't take much interest in things in her life growing up. She loved makeup and shopping. She planned her prom night when she was nine. I just wanted to read all the time, and I avoided boys for the most part. I was close to marrying my best friend; we even got engaged. He was going into the military and wanted the extra benefits."

"What happened? Obviously you didn't go through with it."

"He fractured his back playing football. The army would no longer take him, so we called off the wedding. I think he was even more relieved than I was."

"Have you told your parents that you're gay?" Jules was curious.

"Oh, my, no. They would ship me off to Zimbabwe if they ever found out. My dad is a preacher and my mom teaches Sunday school. They are mad enough that we both work in a bar. If Melinda tells them, I'll never speak to her again and she knows it. What about you? Any siblings?"

"I have four brothers and three sisters. My mom died when I was fourteen, so we're a pretty close-knit group."

"Eight kids, damn. Any of them know you're gay?"

"Well, my oldest sister is gay and I suspect that my youngest brother is. I have never said anything because, well, honestly, I've never acted on it. I've pretty much lost myself in school. Dad couldn't pay for college for eight kids, so I had to earn a scholarship. I've never taken the time to look, much less date. Well, then you caught my eye." Jules winked.

Just then the waiter arrived with two more drinks and a bowl of bar nuts. "Compliments of the ladies at the bar."

"Thanks." Jules looked over and saw Sam laughing. She tried to catch Sam's attention, but she was too far into hysterics.

"Oh, that's just not funny." Sarah grinned.

"Well, something is funny. Have you been listening to them?"

Sarah turned around to look. "That was them all night? I thought it was the group of frat guys over there making all that noise. Are you gonna eat the nuts?"

"Well, I'm sure they're fresh in this place. I love cashews and I am feeling a little snacky." Jules inspected the bowl. "I'll eat them if you do."

Sarah popped two almonds in her mouth. "We should thank them. Try to get their attention."

Jules waved a few times to no avail. Finally, she picked up a cashew and hurled it across the bar. "I can't believe I just did that."

"Did you hit anyone?" Sarah was clearly impressed.

"No one important. Just the owner of the Laine Hotel. Oh, shit, they're coming over."

Sam approached the table and joked, "Um, we're gonna have to ask you ladies to leave. There is a strict policy in this bar that food is not to become airborne."

"We were just trying to get your attention." Sarah clearly thought she was serious, but Jules smiled.

"Well, then that's okay. But if I have a permanent moon shape on my forehead, I may have to sue. Maybe next time, just shout or whistle really loud."

"I didn't think you'd be able to hear us. Some ladies at the bar are being very disruptive and loud." Jules shook her head.

"Oh, touché. I guess we'll all have to behave then." Sam pulled up a chair. "Mind if we join you for a bit?"

"Not at all, Miss Laine. Our table is your table." Jules made a sweeping gesture.

"I'm picking up the literal meaning in that. So who gave me away? The bartender?"

"Front desk. We canceled one of the rooms." Sarah obviously spoke without thinking and Jules gave her a warning look.

"Oh, my. Thanks to the clerk's big mouth, the hotel will have a position to fill. And speaking of positions—" Sam stopped, knowing that the double entendre was inappropriate. "Actually, we should probably let you have your privacy."

Sarah said, "Oh, please join us. It would be our pleasure."

Jules seemed to like the fact that Sarah was already using the word *our* and speaking for the both of them.

Doc said, "That's fine. Sam, I need your office key. I want to get some cigarettes."

Sam passed her a set of keys. They waited a few minutes for her to be out of earshot.

"Is everything okay? We didn't figure on seeing you guys again tonight."

Sam played with the label on her beer bottle. "Her sister doesn't have much time left. She talked to her brother and will be heading down to Houston on Monday."

"She seems to be handling it okay." Sarah was whispering.

"I don't know that she is. In all the time I've known her, I've never seen her cry. It seems that she lets herself go through laughter. You probably noticed, of course. I cannot imagine what she's going through, but she won't talk to me. I'm hoping she will let me in soon. I'm afraid she's going to explode."

"Does her sister live in Houston?" Sara asked.

"No. She lives in Montana, but there is a doctor down there who was highly recommended so Doc and her brother flew Amy down there. They wanted the best for her, of course."

"Of course." Sarah sighed. "Poor Doc."

"I remember when my mom died," Jules began, "I had no idea how I was supposed to act. I was angry and scared. I was lucky, though. It was sudden. She was in an accident. I didn't get to say good-bye, but it probably would have been harder on us kids if we did have to say good-bye and watch her suffer."

Sarah took Jules's hand. "Man, can you imagine what it would be like to lose a twin? Twins have such a deeper bond than most siblings."

"I never met Amy. They talk on the phone a lot; they seem really tight. I'm not even sure her family knows about me, with the exception of Jack." Sam glanced around the room. "I have a feeling that Doc's not coming back to the bar. I'd better go find her. You girls enjoy the room. You're welcome to stay the weekend."

"I have to work tomorrow." Sarah moaned. "But thank you so much for everything."

"Yeah, thanks. Tell Doc not to worry, that I got the classes covered. Maybe she could just call me on Sunday if she has any instructions?"

"I'll tell her. Thanks. 'Night." Sam gave them each a kiss on the cheek and left.

"Baby, are you asleep?" Sam curled up beside me on the bed.

"No, just thinking."

"Whatcha thinking about?"

"I was in your office. I saw that picture you have of me on your desk."

"Uh-huh." She stroked my hair.

"For a second, I thought it was a picture of Amy."

"I'm sorry, Dani." She sighed. "Are you okay?"

"I just want to sleep. Please can I just sleep?"

"Of course you can. I'm here if you need me. I love you."

I couldn't open my mouth to respond. I lay there for an hour listening to her breathe and wondered why I couldn't cry in front of her. Every once in a while I felt her stroke my hair or my back. I could feel how much she loved me, but I couldn't let myself be loved by anyone ever again.

On the elevator ride to the seventh floor, Jules could feel the heat of Sarah's body next to hers. The five-foot gap that had separated them six hours earlier was closed to a mere six inches. The appetizers at the bar were enough to keep the two of them from getting overly tipsy. The only thing buzzing in Jules's mind was the unbelievable want of a woman's touch, and the only woman she wanted was Sarah.

They settled into the room quickly, each taking turns playing with all the gadgets.

"Are you tired?" Sarah asked while settling into the recliner.

"You'd think I would be. It seems like forever ago that we were talking about Jell-O wrestling. I'm actually pretty wide awake, considering. Are you tired?"

"A little. I think two days of drinking has worn me out." Sarah stifled a yawn.

"Well, you should get some sleep. I'll probably watch a little TV. What time do you need to be home?"

"I don't work until four, so as long as I'm home by midafternoon, I should be okay." She got up and went into the bathroom. "Would you believe that there are toothbrushes and Laine Hotel pajamas in here?"

"Man, the people who can afford suites have it made." Jules got up to look.

"Either that or Sam thought of everything for us. There are even slippers and robes."

Sarah brushed her teeth and put on the new cotton pajamas. She checked herself in the mirror and realized how tired she looked. She worried that Jules would never touch her if she looked so sleepy. She splashed some cold water on her face and ran a comb through her hair. When she finally went back into the room, Jules was already asleep on the sofa. *Bummer,* she thought and grabbed a blanket from the closet. As gently as she could, she lay the blanket over Jules's relaxed body. A chill went up her spine and she was plagued with a feeling she had never felt before. She leaned down and put her face close to the face of her new friend. Before she could help herself, she pressed her lips against Jules's.

She was exhilarated to feel the kiss reciprocated. Jules awoke from her slumber and placed her hands on Sarah's hips. Gently, she pulled Sarah down to her side and kissed her with all the passion and heat Sarah had dreamed of. She didn't know if anything more than a kiss was in their future, but that one sweet kiss had been worth the wait. Sarah could feel how much Jules wanted her, and she wanted Jules just as badly. She realized at that moment that she didn't want to be loved by anyone else, except Jules, ever again.

Chapter Six

The next morning I found myself yelling at Sam. "You're going back to California. It's decided, no discussion."

"I am not going back to school. I am going with you to Houston."

"I need to do this on my own. I need to concentrate on Amy and my family."

"I want to be there for you, Doc. I want to help you through this." She was practically in tears.

"This is not the time for me to be explaining to my family who you are. You know I haven't told them about us yet. My parents have enough to worry about without having to face the disappointing lifestyle of their surviving daughter."

"So you'd rather go through this alone than tell them I'm your girlfriend?"

"Yes." I was too tired to argue. Part of me wanted her to be mad at me so she would just leave. I wanted to be left alone, and I was annoyed that she couldn't see that this was a personal journey for me.

"So what happens next time there's a crisis? Are you going to send me across the country then too?" She was definitely yelling.

"One crisis at a time, Sam. Don't you get it? I don't want you there!" It took every ounce of strength that I had to say that. Every muscle in my body tensed as I felt myself yell at this beautiful woman. I had never fought tears and anger so hard in my life.

"Okay. That's all you had to say." She stared at the floor for a few minutes then called the front desk. "Tim, it's Samantha Laine. Send someone up for my bags. Tell Jerry that I need a ride to the airport. Twenty minutes. Yes. Thank you."

"Sam." I didn't know what to say. I had enough good-byes to deal with and I hoped that this one, at least, wasn't permanent. "I hope you understand."

"Don't worry. I understand."

"I can take you to the airport." The guilt was already setting in.

"No. You need to go home and pack. Are you sure you can make the drive to Houston? You could hop on Southwest Airlines."

"No, I can make it. It's only five hours. I'll need my car down there anyway to run Mom and Dad around." I was already dreading the whole scenario.

"Okay. Well, let me know where you are staying. Call me if you need me. If I don't answer, page me. I can be back in Texas in no time at all." She started crying again.

"Okay, dreamer. Thanks for—" I choked. "Have a safe trip. Call me when you get in."

She leaned in and gave me a soft, slow kiss. Despite all the anguish I felt, her kiss still stirred my insides. I knew that this good-bye wasn't forever. I knew that when all this was over, my life and all my crises would be with Sam by my side.

"I love you, Dani."

"I love you too." It felt so good to say it and truly mean it.

Sarah woke up Saturday with a headache and chapped lips. It took her a few minutes to replay the prior evening's events in her mind. The highlight, of course, being the two hours of exploration she and Jules shared in the wee hours of the morning. Nothing too major, but enough to leave her satisfied. She smiled and rolled over to find a messy-haired, snoring woman by her side. She felt practically giddy and wanted to get up and dance. Instead she tiptoed across the floor and sat down with the room service menu. A few minutes later, she saw a note slide under the door.

Ladies,

I hope you enjoyed your night in Dallas. As I said, you are welcome to stay the weekend.

Should you decide to leave, please try to check out by one to make the room available for others. I'm flying back to California earlier than planned. Please check on Doc before you go. She may need a ride home. Our room is extension 2011. Also, Jules, please touch base with her tomorrow. I am sure she has some instructions for you regarding school and may forget to call. It was great to hang with you, and we look forward to doing it again.

Thanks,

Sam

P.S. The egg white omelet is extraordinary.

"Mmmm. Good morning." Jules stretched looked at the clock. It was already ten.

"Hey, sleepyhead."

"Did I snore?"

"Just a tad." Sarah held up the slip of paper. "We got a note from Sam. She's kicking us out. Apparently you were so loud that the entire seventh floor complained."

"What!?" Jules blushed and retreated under the covers until she heard Sarah laugh. "Ha ha, very funny. What did the note really say?"

"It said to order an omelet, be out by one and call Doc before we go. Maybe offer her a ride home."

"Okay, why did she leave a note? She could have called."

"Probably didn't want to wake us. She probably heard you snoring through the door. It says she's already heading back to California."

"No way. I can't believe she would just leave Doc. That's pretty harsh, given everything that's going on. I would never leave you with something that major going on." Jules realized the commitment she had just made. "I mean, I could never leave . . ."

"It's okay. I know what you meant. I couldn't leave you either." She stared at Jules for a minute, then suddenly seemed to snap back to reality. "So, should we order room service, or do you want to go downstairs for breakfast?"

"I'm a little shy about someone bringing us food. They'll see two women, one bed, and I'll panic."

"Well, you'd better get used to it. Besides, I'm sure, given their boss, that the people here are used to two women in one bed." Sarah seemed a bit annoyed. "But there was a cute place over on the strip. We could get dressed and walk over there. You could even hold my hand over coffee and no one would bat an eye."

"That sounds great. Should we call and invite Doc?" She reached for the phone.

"Of course." Sarah gave her the extension number.

Jules dialed and Doc answered on the first ring, but she declined their invitation for breakfast.

"Tell her that it's our treat," Sarah interjected.

Jules conveyed Sarah's remark, but Doc still said no. She also declined the offer of a ride home.

"She's not interested?" Sarah seemed a little disappointed.

"She said she's headed to get some things from her brother's house, and then she's heading home to pack. She reminded me that Sam would pay for breakfast at the hotel, but I told her we wanted to see the strip."

"She didn't want us to drive her home?"

"No, she pointed out that we all couldn't fit in my truck anyway. She asked me to house-sit while she's gone—she's got a cat. I'm gonna go over at noon tomorrow and get the tour."

"That's cool. Damn, you're taking over her job and her house. If only you could take over her girlfriend's income, then we'd be set."

"True. Man, I feel kinda bad. She sounds terrible." Jules thought about how tired she sounded. "I wonder if they had a fight. Maybe that's why Sam left. I'd hate to think of them breaking up. They're perfect together."

"Yeah. I'm sure they're fine. There's gotta be a reason Sam left. It's just weird that she left today instead of Sunday like she said she was going to."

The phone rang.

"Hello? . . . Oh, we're fine. All that stuff was in the room. Yeah, Sam thinks of everything. We really appreciate it . . . Yeah, she left a note . . . Oh, we were wondering . . . No, of course not . . . I totally understand . . . Okay, Doc. Take care."

"She change her mind?" Sarah was hopeful.

"No, she wanted to make sure we had toiletries and offered a change of clothes."

"Damn, thoughtful in a crisis, she's good people."

"Very good. She wanted to explain about Sam's leaving. She didn't want us to think less of Sam."

"Oh? What'd she say?"

"That she told Sam to go back today. That she didn't want to have to explain the relationship to her family, and that they are still together."

"Man, I wonder when it is that we all finally tell our families everything. They've been together quite a while. Sam said that she never even met Amy. Could you imagine?"

"Yeah, that's gotta be tough on both of them."

It was weird to go into my brother's house when he wasn't there. He lived in East Dallas about twenty minutes from the Laine Hotel. He had a great old house that he was always updating. I walked around and looked at all his new toys. He was an electronics junkie and always had the latest TV equipment. After digging through several shelves and dressers, I finally found the photo album he asked for. The box marked "Twins" was right where he said it would be. I wasn't sure why my brother would have a box filled with our things, and I was intrigued. It was taped shut, so I decided not to open it until I was with Amy. I knew if I came across some wonderful memorabilia, I would be in tears the rest of the day.

I'd decided to raid his fridge rather than stopping for lunch. I kinda wished I'd gone to breakfast with the girls, but I didn't want to be any more of a downer on their first weekend together. I was a bit nostalgic remembering my first weekend with Sam. If those girls had half the connection that Sam and I had, they would be in for a wild ride. I found some bologna and bread and settled in front of the enormously large television. The phone rang, and I let the answering machine get it.

"This is the residence of Dr. Jackson O'Connor. If you are calling regarding a dental emergency, please call my office." His message went on and finally the beep sounded.

"Jack, it's Sam. I think I've dialed your home instead of your cell. I'll try the other number. Doc sent me back like you thought she would. Please keep in touch and let me know what I can do. Please take care of her for me. I know how hard all of this is for you. I am so sorry." She started crying. "Okay, I'll try the other number. Please call me back in Cali. Or you can page me. I love you, Jack. It's gonna be okay. Okay, 'bye."

I had no idea that Jack and Sam were so close. I knew that they had lunch once in a while when I was teaching. The depth of the concern in her voice toward my brother was surprising. I suddenly felt so bad that I didn't let her in with the rest of my family before now. I realized then that my own selfishness deprived Amy of knowing someone as wonderful as Sam. It deprived my sister of seeing how happy I was. And it deprived Sam of meeting the other half of me. It meant that Sam would never understand fully why I am the way I am. Sam was a member of a family she'd never met. Sam really wanted to be with me during all this. I sat in front of the monstrosity of a television and cried. It was too late.

Jules rang the doorbell right at noon on Sunday, just as promised. I had nearly forgotten she was coming by. My house was a complete disaster and I hadn't showered. I'd been up all night poring through boxes, trying to find a measly stuffed dog that Amy won at the state fair when we were fourteen. I climbed over stacks of books, piles of photos and mounds of old clothes to make my way to the door.

"Hey, Jules. Thanks for coming by."

"Hi. Is this a bad time?" She looked at the mess behind me.

"No, come on in. Sorry about the clutter—just step over it." I held the door open wide. "I'll try to have it all cleaned up before I leave tomorrow."

"Oh, I forgot you were leaving tomorrow. I thought it was today. I brought my stuff and was ready to start."

"No. Tomorrow, Monday." I sighed. "Sorry about that."

"No problem. I could help you pack all this back up." She motioned to the piles.

My first instinct was to decline. Then I realized that I couldn't spend another night looking at my memories. "You know what, that would be great. In fact, could you stay tonight and keep me company, since you're already ready and all?" I didn't want to be alone and was kicking myself for sending Sam away.

"Sure. I'd be happy to. Where should we start?"

"The clothes. Just grab a box and throw all this shit into it. Want some coffee?"

"Okay, sure. Cream or milk, no sugar." She was folding my old concert T-shirts. "Man, these are retro. You've got Foreigner, Stray Cats, Depeche Mode, Genesis, even the Pretenders. You must have been to a lot of concerts."

"Yeah. Amy used to come visit me when I was a student. We would catch every concert that Dallas had to offer. It was so funny because Amy used to—" I stopped, unable to go on.

"Amy used to what?" She followed me into the kitchen. "Doc?"

"Amy used to try to go backstage," I whispered.

"I'm sorry. I didn't mean to bring up sad memories." I could tell she felt bad.

"No, the memories aren't sad. It's just that there won't be any more concerts for us. There won't be any more new memories for Amy and me." I started sobbing. "This is crazy. I can't shed a tear in front of my own girlfriend. Then you come over, and two minutes later I'm Niagara Falls."

"You probably just don't want to be vulnerable in front of Sam. You're supposed to be the strong one and take care of her. She is a bit of a delicate flower, despite the sarcastic exterior. You probably think she needs you more than you need her. It's okay. You can get through this whether you cry in front of your girl-friend or not."

"Boy, I hope so. I'm a total mess." I dried my eyes and re-gained my train of thought. "Okay, coffee, cream and no sugar. You know what? Take those concert shirts and put them on my bed. I think I will pack them, and Amy and I can wear them this week."

"That's a great idea." She took the stack of faded black shirts down the hall.

By six o'clock we finished cleaning up the house and sat on the back deck. I ordered her a pizza but couldn't make myself eat. We chatted about classes and I felt comfortable with her filling in for me. We talked about Sarah, and how the rest of their time to-gether was spent. Jules was definitely gay, she told me. There were no mistakes, and no need for that aforementioned nunnery. We talked about Sam, and the hotel and the Dallas strip. Not once did we discuss our families, let alone our siblings, although she did mention that she had seven. I was awed and jealous. Finally I could no longer keep my eyes open and started for bed.

"Hey, Doc," she said softly. "There is a pink elephant in the room."

"I know." I knew what she meant.

"I'll listen if you want to talk about it."

"I just don't know what to expect. I don't know what state she's in. It's hard when you're twins, because we used to look so much alike. I'm afraid I'll see myself as ill, because I have always looked at Amy like I'm looking at a mirror image."

"That's understandable to be afraid. No one wants to try to be strong when they're in a position they've never been in before. But you have to remember that no one knows how to act, and no one is more scared than Amy."

"That's true. I just don't want her to read my fear on my face."

"See, you made an interesting point, Doc. You said you look at her like she's a mirror image, and you're afraid of how sick she may look."

"Right."

"Well, don't you think she's always seen you as her mirror image? You look strong and healthy. She may feel better or stronger just looking at you. So it's not that you need to be afraid of how she looks. You need to make sure that you reflect that image for her that she needs to see. Well, I didn't word it well, but you know what I mean?"

"Yes. I hadn't thought of that. It's funny because she was the more outgoing one, and the wild one. I always looked at her to be our 'twin representative.' I guess now I need to be the strong, outgoing one."

"Right. And one more thing. If you don't mind me giving you a little advice."

"No, please do. Although you have already given me great insight, Jules. Shoot."

"After my mom died, I was a total disaster. I couldn't pull myself together. I mourned for years. Finally, one day my aunt pulled me aside and told me to snap out of it. She said my sadness wasn't helping my family heal, not my father, my brothers or my sisters. It made me realize that there is a time to mourn. That time for you may be before Amy passes, or it may be for years after. But there is a time to mourn and there is a time to let go." She shrugged. "That advice may mean nothing to you now, but you might remember those words later, and they may help you."

"Thanks, Jules. I'll try to remember that. I'm sorry about your mom." Her words didn't have much meaning for me, but I tucked them in the back of my mind for later use. "I'm glad you're here." I started to walk into the house then stopped. I turned around and kissed Jules on the forehead. "You're mom would have been proud of you. You're a great kid."

"You're a great kid too, Doc. See you in the morning."

Chapter Seven

I thought about staying at Houston's Laine Hotel, but it was so far away from the cancer hospital that it wouldn't have made sense. I checked into a Ramada late Monday night, the same hotel where my mom was staying. I made no effort to go to the hospital or to try and see my mom when I got in. I lay awake all night listening to the sounds of traffic and the neighboring ice machine. I had a wake-up call for six and checked the clock every five minutes.

Finally, at 5:48, the dreaded phone rang. *Early*, I thought.

"Hello?"

"Doc? Are you sleeping?"

"Mom?"

"No, baby, it's Sam."

"I thought it was my wake-up call."

"Well, if I woke you, then it is." She laughed.

"It's, like, four o'clock there. Why are you up?"

"I wanted to talk to you before you went to the hospital."

"Did you just get up, or have you been up all night?" I don't know why I asked.

"I just got up. I couldn't really sleep. I was worried about you."

"I didn't sleep much either. The Ramada isn't as comfortable as the Laine."

"Well, I'm sure the Ramada has its upside." She never insulted the competition. "I just had a few things I thought you should know before you began your day."

"Okay." *Great, more advice*, I thought.

"You're an amazing, independent woman. I know you don't need me there to hold your hand because I know you'll be strong enough on your own. You refer to Amy as your other half, and I totally understand why. But please remember that you are your own person, your own spirit and your own soul as well." It sounded like she had rehearsed the words.

"I know." Tears streamed down my face but I didn't let on.

"You've touched the lives of so many people—your family, your students and especially me. You make me look forward to every single day. Don't let Amy's being sick make you forget who you are on your own." She paused. "I'm sure that when you come into a world with a twin, you assume she'll be with you for your entire life. Just remember that Amy will always be a part of you, forever. You will carry on, and the legacy that you leave in this world will be her legacy too. Don't be scared, or ashamed of who you are. You are the most amazing soul I have ever met, and I, like so many others, am proud to be a part of your life."

"Thank you, Sammy." It was all I could say.

"I don't know if I've ever told you this, but I love you more than anything. You are truly loved, and your love is felt by me.

I'll stay out here until the minute you call me home. But please remember that I am here and ready to get on a plane at any time. You don't have to protect me, or us, or anyone. You just have to do what feels right to you."

"Okay, Sammy." Again, it was all I could think to say.

"Okay, Doc. I know you need to go. I'll let you go."

"Okay, Sammy." My voice shook.

A half-hour later, I squeezed myself into a white J. Geils Band T-shirt. It fit a lot better eighteen years earlier. I stopped for doughnuts and cappuccino and made my way to the hospital. Before I walked into Amy's room, I took a deep breath and plastered on a fake smile.

"Dani! It's about fuckin' time."

"Hey, Ames. How's it going?" I couldn't help but grin for real when I saw her. Even though she was so thin and pale, she still looked like me—like us. She was wearing a Cowboys jersey and a Redskins cap. "Looks like you're still the noncommittal football fan."

"Hell, I like the 'Skins' defense and the 'Boys' offense. What can ya do? I am so glad you're here. If I had to spend one more day with Mom, I would have died of boredom before the cancer got me." She reached for a chocolate-covered doughnut. "Oh, thank God. The food here is shit on a shingle. For fuck's sakes, even on death row they let you choose your last meal."

"My, you've become quite the potty mouth." I was already tired of the death references.

"Well, life's short. Jack told Mom that the drugs were making me swear. I'm just doing it on purpose because I like watching the old bag cringe every time she hears the F bomb."

"Going out with a bang, huh, Ames?" Before it came out I regretted it.

"Okay, I'm the only one who can make death remarks." She continued to smile. "You look great. If I didn't know better, I'd guess you were in love."

"Ah, what do you know." I offered her another doughnut.

"Jack mentioned a Sam. Am I to assume that's the reason for your youthful appearance and glow?"

"Nah, I got stoned in the parking lot. That explains the glow. So, did your friends already head back to Billings?" I tried to steer the conversation before I had to play the pronoun game.

"Yeah, they left this morning. That was a bitch. It's so surreal to see how people react in a time like this."

"Well, everyone is different. How do you want them to act?" I prayed she had the answer.

"I guess if people weren't sad, it would mean they didn't like me. But you know what?"

"What?"

"As much as everyone hates to see me go, I hate it even more. I've gotten used to my life. Guess I kinda wanted to see how it turned out. I feel like I'm a TV show that got canceled halfway through the season."

"Boy, that's a deep analogy. Couldn't you come up with something a little more romantic?"

"Ain't nothing romantic about death, Danielle. I've spent the last year puking and sleeping and going bald. I smell, I hurt and I'm angry. Now the time has come for me to move on, and do you know what I get?"

"What do you get?" Apprehensive, I sat on the edge of the bed.

"I get a week, maybe two, of watching the people that I love be miserable. And I can't run away from it or hide. I am stuck in this damn bed while you all get to go cry in the waiting room. I feel so guilty knowing what I'm putting you all through. But, Jesus, it would be nice if I could spend my last precious moments here on earth having some fun. It'd be great if everyone didn't look at me with those 'pity faces.' 'Oh, poor Amy, boo-hoo.'" She rolled her eyes.

"Well, you're in luck. I'm not here to pity you, and I'm not here to cry. I'm not even here to say good-bye. I have a carload of photographs and board games. I've arranged for a DVD player and I've rented some movies. So save your breath. You don't need to tell me what you want. I'm your twin. I can read your mind."

I decided then and there that I wasn't going to be sad. I was going to make her last bit of time into one last good memory for the both of us.

"Oh, yeah? What am I thinking right now?"

"Let's see. All the machines are throwing me off, but either you want another doughnut or you have to fart." I closed my eyes like I was in deep thought.

"Bingo!"

"Which one?"

She passed gas and grabbed another doughnut. "Both."

We sat and talked for about three hours. I could tell she was really tired but refused to sleep while I was there. Around noon I lied and told her that I had some phone calls to make. She was asleep before I even left the room. I went to the waiting room and called Jack first and then my parents. I told them everything the doctor told me, which wasn't much different than what Jack had already said, except that I learned that Amy's time was more limited than we thought. There was one thing that Jack hadn't mentioned, which was a major worry for me. It seemed that Amy didn't have insurance. She was self-employed and never bothered to get health coverage. By the time she got around to inquiring, it was too late. The cancer was a preexisting condition. I knew Jack didn't want me to stress about the bills, but I knew it was a matter that we had to resolve, and the sooner the better.

I called Jack back and asked him what he thought we could do about it. I figured the final bills, plus the funeral, would surpass a hundred and fifty thousand dollars. He said he planned on coming up with the money. His dental practice was still in the pioneering stage, but he was sure he could have all of Amy's medical bills paid within five or six years. We knew there was no way that our parents would be able to help. Dad was working really hard to save for retirement. It wouldn't be good for his health to have to work another ten years to cover the bills. Amy wouldn't have much of an estate. She lived in a rental house and was making car payments. We figured that what she had in savings was probably already used up on previous bills over the last year.

I told Jack that it wasn't up to him to pay all the bills. He, of course, argued, reminding me what I made on my teacher's salary. After much deliberation, we reached an agreement that he and I would divide all the expenses fifty-fifty. I think he was relieved, as it was important for him to start saving for his own office, rather than the rental he was in. I wished I was in a situation where I could have taken the entire burden instead of just half. I felt a responsibility toward my sister. I was there when she was born—hell, I was there before she was born. I wanted to be there one hundred percent when she left.

"Sam?" I'd called Sam's cell phone three times and hung up each time. I was trying to get the courage to talk to her about money and not let on how scared I was.

"Yes. Oh, hey, Doc. How's it going?" She seemed to sound intentionally casual.

"It's going okay. Amy told me what she expects of me this week, and I have vowed to honor her request."

"And what was that?"

"Just to make her last hours fun and memorable. No tears, no good-byes."

"Can you handle that?" Her casualness turned to concern.

"I'm starting to think I can handle anything."

"I'm glad to hear that."

"Man, Amy doesn't have any health insurance."

"Oh, shit. I was afraid of that. Self-employed people rarely do when they first start out."

"Jack and I are going to each take half the burden. But there's a problem, baby."

"I already know, Doc. It's okay. This is far more important. The house can wait."

"I'm sorry. Can you call the realtor and call off the search?"

"Of course I can. Don't be sorry. I totally understand." Her voice was calming. "Doc, we've been searching for a house together this long, we can wait. We have all the time in the world."

"Can you transfer half the money out of our joint savings into my personal account?"

"You got it." She was my rock.

"Boy, that's my entire life's savings."

"Well, it's Amy's life you're thinking about today. It's the right thing to do."

"Thanks for not offering to pay Amy's bills or cover the down payment on the house."

"Doc, I figure you know that the offer is a given. You know I would do it in a heartbeat. But I know how important it is for you to pay for your own sister's care. I would never stand in the way of your doing what you feel is right."

"Thanks. I'll call you tonight."

"I'm in class until seven, Houston time. Page me if you need to."

"'Kay. Gotta run. Thanks."

"You betcha."

I dawdled around the area for a while going in and out of a few local shops. I came across a great deal on DVDs, so I picked up a dozen—mainly comedies and a couple of Hitchcock classics. I stumbled into a flower shop and thought that it was too ordinary and morbid to bring her flowers, especially knowing that they might outlive the patient. My heart sank as I wondered, *how can she only have a week to live?* I settled on a balloon bouquet, with the intent of sucking out the helium and making dwarf voices. I stopped by an art supply store and got some pastels and paper. Amy had been a pretty good artist when we were in high school.

When I got back to the hospital, I was completely loaded down. An intern with a wheelchair spotted me and offered to wheel my goods in for me. I felt pretty weird about the vast number of balloons but explained to him that they were for entertainment more than just show. He understood but felt the need to remind me about the side effects of ingesting helium. I had no idea, really, that it was that dangerous.

I got up to the third floor, and my mom was standing outside Amy's room.

"Hey, stranger. I didn't plan on seeing you until dinner." I set down my goodies.

"I came by to bring my girls some cookies." She gave me a tight hug. "But they wouldn't let me in."

"What?" I immediately started to panic. "I was here all morning. She seemed okay."

"I know. She was in great spirits with me and her friends yesterday. She was very alert and appeared to be her normal, aggressive self. Oh, she's so thin." Mom started to cry just as the doctor came out of Amy's room.

"We've given her a little more for the pain. Her blood pressure is down. She's obviously weak." He put some notes on a chart.

"I thought you said she was doing okay. I thought you said two weeks," my mom practically yelled.

"Shhh. Sometimes this happens. When patients start to experience closure, they start to slide a bit. She is obviously fighting, but honestly, at this rate, I'd have to say it's more like a matter of days."

I felt so guilty. Maybe I was the closure she was waiting for. Maybe she was hanging on to see me one last time. "Is there anything that can be done?"

"It's just time. We are doing everything we can. I suggest that you call in the family now and prepare yourselves." He started down the hall.

"Dad comes in tomorrow?" I asked my mom.

She nodded. "Yes. And Jack on Thursday."

"I'll call Jack in a bit and tell him to fly down tonight. I'm going in. Are you coming?"

"No, I think I need to call your father and let this sink in. I don't want to lose it in front of her. I'll be there in a few." She squeezed my arm and headed down the hall.

I pushed the intern's wheelchair into my sister's room. "Damn, Ames. I leave for two hours and they hand out the good drugs?"

"Yeah, you missed the Jell-O too." She even sounded different. "What did you bring me?"

"I have balloons, pastels and movies. I also have a photo album and a box of junk that Jack was saving for us. I have no idea what's in it. What do you want to play with first?"

"Actually, I'd like to talk for a bit." She sounded too serious for a woman who wanted her last precious moments to be fun.

"Okay, what's the topic?" I carefully crawled into bed next to her.

"I want to confess a few things."

"I'm hardly a priest and you're hardly Catholic, Miss Potty Mouth."

"There's just some things that I'd like to get off my chest. You're my soul mate, the only soul mate I've ever known or ever will know." She lay her head on my shoulder.

"I'm listening." I stroked her arm and noticed how frail she was.

"I never got my doctorate."

"No, but you got your M.B.A."

"But you and Jack have fancy titles, and I'm just 'Miss' or 'Ms.'"

"Well, a fancy title doesn't a good person make. I happen to think that having a master's in business and owning your own company is pretty darned impressive. A lot more impressive than being an English teacher at a woman's college."

"That's true. I totally have you beat in the world of success." Her breathing was labored.

"What else you got?"

"I don't have anything to leave you. I mean, you're welcome to my clothes, my car payment, my golf clubs and my jewelry. But I don't have anything significant to give you to remember me by."

"I don't need anything to remember you by. I have all our memories. Almost every happy moment of my life was spent with you. My entire childhood revolved around you. You'll be a part of me forever, and I'll think of you every single day for the rest of my life."

"Please think of me fondly." She laughed.

"I always do. Well, except for that time in the tenth grade when you kissed my boyfriend. I'll be sure to try and forget about that memory."

"He didn't like you, Dani. He was dating you to get to me. A week later he was dating our cousin."

"Our cousin? Sylvia?"

"No. James."

I had to laugh. "Oh, that explains a lot."

"Dani, do something important. I never did anything important in my life." Amy sighed.

"That's not true. Your life has impacted so many people. So many people love you." Suddenly I remembered what Sam said on the phone that morning: *The legacy you leave will be her legacy too*. "But I promise that I'll make you proud."

Amy took a deep breath and relaxed. After a few minutes, I could tell she was sleeping again, but I checked her heart monitor to be sure. I slowly slipped off the bed and tiptoed out of the room. When I got to the hallway, I leaned back against the wall and stared at the floor. Without realizing it, I had slid down the wall and was sitting on the cold floor sobbing harder than ever in my life.

I knew I needed to call Jack, so I forced myself to take a deep breath and calm down. My hands shook as I dialed.

The phone was answered on the first ring. "Dental office. May I help you?"

"Dr. O'Connor, please."

"He's with a patient. May I give him a message?" The voice was too jovial.

"It's kind of an emergency."

"Well, you can come into the office, or I can let you speak to his assistant."

"It's not a tooth emergency. It's a family emergency."

"Well, I can take a note into him. May I ask who is calling?"

"Get my fucking brother on the phone right now or I will reach through this phone and extract your molars!" That was the point when I realized I was a little angry.

Two minutes passed.

"Dani? What's going on? Betty's in tears." I couldn't tell if the concern in his voice was for me or for his receptionist.

"I'm sorry. Tell Betty I'm sorry."

"Okay. What is it?"

"It's time, Jack. You need to come down." My voice rasped.

"Thursday's not soon enough?"

"Jack, you need to get down here, you need to fly, and you need to leave right now."

"Oh, my God. Okay. I need to finish this crown. Southwest goes every half-hour. I'll try to get on the two thirty."

"Try to get on the two. I'll pick you up." My voice was stronger.

"No, you stay there. I'll get a cab. It's gonna be okay, Danielle. I promise." His voice was like stone.

"One day. It's not okay today, Jack. Hurry."

I paged Sam twice and she finally called me back ten minutes later.

"I'm sorry. I had to sneak out of a lecture and wait for a pay phone. My cell doesn't work in these old buildings and it's raining like crazy outside." Sam sounded out of breath.

"It's okay. I'm sorry to drag you out of class. Professors really hate that."

"You would know." She laughed. "Are you okay?"

"I just wanted to hear your voice. I can't really talk. I think I'm going to lose my sister."

"I know, baby. You are. I'm sorry."

"No, I'm going to lose her today." Saying the words aloud made my heart sink.

"Oh. Oh, no. That's fast. Are they sure?"

"They didn't say today exactly. They said a few days. But do you remember that poem I wrote last summer, the one with the two birds flying?"

"Yes, I remember. Oh—the last line."

"'And I will die on a Tuesday.'" I sighed.

"'And I will die on a Tuesday,'" she repeated. "Doc, your poetry can hardly predict the future."

"I know. But I felt it pretty strongly. It's today, Sam. I just know it."

"Oh, boy. I don't know what to tell you."

"Just tell me that you love me."

"I love you with all my heart, Dani."

"I'll call when I can. 'Bye, dreamer."

Chapter Eight

My dad changed his flight and would be in around six. Jack made it on the two o'clock from Dallas and would be at the hospital by four or five. My mom and I sat with Amy and watched her go in and out of sleep. We didn't really talk much; the sound of all the machines made the room seem loud enough. I was feeling faint and remembered that I hadn't eaten much of anything except a doughnut since Friday. I decided to sneak off to the cafeteria to force-feed myself something substantial. The last thing I wanted was to pass out and make everyone panic.

It was the weirdest feeling to be in that hospital. Like Amy had said, it was surreal. There was so much death and sadness in that place that it was haunting. All the visitors looked at one another with such pity and understanding. I had no problem making eye contact with perfect strangers, wondering who it was they were there to lose. I wondered if anyone ever left that place alive, but I didn't care, because it wasn't Amy.

I got a tray full of food—nasty hospital cuisine of macaroni, pudding and vegetables. I sat at a table off in the corner and looked at all the other people sitting by themselves. Normally, I thought, people would sit closer together and maybe even exchange pleasantries. Not in this place. Here everyone wanted to be left alone. This was a place of solitude and a temporary break from the nightmare of the patients' rooms. This was a refuge with soup-colored walls and horrible, punishing food.

I was so relieved to see Jack standing at the door of the cafeteria ten minutes later.

He quietly approached as not to disturb the other cafeteria patrons. "Mom said you were here. Amy's asleep," he whispered as he sat next to me.

"I know. Doesn't that suck. You're at the end of your life and you can't even stay awake long enough to say good-bye." It was an awful observation and I think Jack was stunned.

"I don't think she wants to say good-bye. I think she knows that we love her. We know she loves us. I think it's just a matter of letting nature take its course."

"I haven't told her yet."

"You haven't told her what?" He picked at my macaroni.

"How much she means to me. How much I love her."

"She knows. Did she tell you all that stuff?"

"Not directly." I sniffed.

"But you know she feels that way, right?"

"Yeah. I guess love is a given, huh?" I pushed my tray toward him.

"Yeah. But it wouldn't hurt to say it one last time." He choked on his words.

⊷⊶

For the first time in several years, our family of five was together in one room. Unlike our normal, festive reunions, this one was somber and quiet. I had made a promise to Amy to make this visit fun, but I had to put that promise aside, given the situation. I had also promised that I wouldn't cry; that promise was shot by late morning. The last promise I made was that I wouldn't say good-bye. I wasn't sure if telling her how I felt was the same as a good-bye. I decided that I would say what I needed to say, but I would never use the word *good-bye*.

By ten o'clock that night, Amy was relatively coherent. She was able to make a few jokes and bark a few orders. My dad was supposed to get a haircut every other week. Jack was told to get a wife and have a son. She insisted that my mom learn to laugh a little and swear at least once a week. When I asked what she wanted me to do, she didn't respond. I asked again, and she told me that she would tell me later when no one was around.

With amazing strength, she spoke of her last requests. She wanted to be cremated, and she didn't want an immediate funeral. She wanted us to have a service in December, after Thanksgiving but before Christmas. She figured that it would be the only way we would get together near the holidays. She wanted her ashes spread over the Snowy Range—some mountains near where we grew up in Wyoming, near where my parents live now. I was assigned to keep the ashes until then, and I was supposed to spread them when the time came. She told us that there was a will, and it should be read after the funeral. As far as a living will, she had one—there were to be no heroic measures. I was already aware of that fact. I had signed it months earlier. Finally, she asked to speak to us one at a time, starting with Dad and ending with me. We were to all leave the hospital when she was finished. None of us argued.

Three of us filed out, leaving my dad behind. He was only in her room about ten minutes. He came out looking proud and stoic. He told my mom to meet him in the chapel and they would leave together. He told Jack and me to meet them at the hotel when we were through. He showed no emotion and his steps down the hallway were precise and heavy.

We could hear some music coming from the room as my mom opened the door. I couldn't place the song, but it seemed hauntingly familiar. While she was in there, Jack asked me if I had brought the box from his house. I told him that I had and that it was in Amy's room. He gave me instructions on what I was to do with the contents of the box. I promised I would. We waited for what seemed like an eternity before my mom came out. The door opened and the same song was playing behind her. Like my father, she wasn't crying. She didn't speak a word to us, just kissed us both on the cheek and followed my father's path to the chapel.

Jack paused a minute before he went in. I could tell he was trying to pull himself together. I looked at my watch, 11:08. I knew there wouldn't be much time before she fell asleep again. I took his hand and led him through the door. Amy was sitting upright and smiling. I waved and closed the door behind Jack. As I stood in the hallway, I felt a certain peace come over me, a sense of relief that the pain wouldn't drag on any longer. Not just Amy's pain, but my own pain of worry and guilt. I was reminded of what Jules said to me before I came down here: *There is a time to mourn and a time to let go.* This was my time to let go; I could mourn later.

Jack walked into the hallway with his head down. He looked small, as small as he did when we were kids. "She's really tired, Dani."

"I know." I was nervous, but not sad.

"Everything really is going to be okay, you know?"

"I know, buddy." I gave him a hug.

"I'll meet you outside."

I strolled into the room and saw my pale, thin identical twin propped up on pillows. She was wearing a sweater that my mother had made for her. I recognized the song playing over and over again on her little stereo. It was "Dancing in the Moonlight," a favorite of ours growing up.

"I'm not here to say good-bye, Amy."

"I know." She spoke softly and slowly.

"Can I get you anything?"

"I'm good, but I'm really tired. There were things I wanted to tell you, but I think you already know them all."

"I do. I can read your mind, remember?"

"That's right." She laughed. "Are you happy, Doc? Do you have a good life?"

"I do. I am very happy in my life."

"Have you found someone to love?"

"I have. But you will always be my soul mate." I touched her hand.

"We were together at the very beginning—" She stopped and I prayed she wouldn't finish the sentence.

"That's right. The O'Connor twins. It's been a wild ride, Amy."

"Yeah. I told you I had one request that I would tell you later."

"Yes, you did."

"I want you to be free, Danielle. I want you to laugh, and love, and enjoy every moment of your life. I want you to loosen up, drop your inhibitions and be free."

"I can do that. I will do that. I promise." I stroked her cheek.

"And you can't cry. Not here, not tonight. You guys all go back to the hotel, and you drink a toast to me. Then you go outside and look at the stars. And you spend the rest of your lives happy and free."

"I promise."

She tried to talk some more, but the words weren't coming. I remembered what Jack said about the box. I pulled the tape off and removed the contents. Inside were two blankets. My stomach sank. The two baby blankets that our mother had made for us before we were even born. I placed her baby blanket over her legs and wrapped mine around my shoulders. She was trying so hard to stay awake and to speak.

The last words that Sam said on the phone to me that morning played in my head. I kissed Amy on the forehead and repeated those words. "I know you need to go. I'll let you go."

Amy Elizabeth O'Connor died at 11:57 P.M. on a Tuesday. It was a warm April night, three months after our birthday and eight months before her funeral. Amy was a small-town girl, with an amazing heart and a beautiful smile—my smile, my heart, my soul. No one in my family cried the night Amy died. Instead, we drank a toast and danced in the moonlight.

Chapter Nine

I went back to work the following Monday. Sam and I decided that it would be best for her to stay out West until the semester ended. Well, I should say that I decided, and she argued for two days before she agreed. I can't say that things were back to normal, because in my mind nothing would ever be normal again. I would be struck, at the oddest times, with a penetrating sense of emptiness. I tried to fill the void with work, writing, painting, sleeping, eating and drinking. Nothing worked. No matter how hard I tried to distract myself, I was still completely lost.

I managed to put up a good front. On the outside I was a bit goofier than normal and spent a little more time with friends and students. On the inside, I was critically wounded and saw no healing in sight. The self-medication of alcohol, which had worked so many times in the past, didn't seem to numb me. The thrill of reading a new book or discovering an old movie was no longer thrilling. The anticipation I usually felt at the end of each semester wasn't there this time. I didn't care that my favorite seniors were graduating, and I didn't look forward to my short summer vacation.

One evening in May during the last week of classes, I sat on my back deck grading finals. I thought I heard a scratching noise at my fence. I sat and listened and heard nothing. A few minutes later, I heard a clinking sound like bottles. Again, I sat still and listened and heard nothing. About half an hour passed before I heard music coming from my living room. My heart pounded and I looked around for a weapon. I thought maybe my cat stepped on my CD player, but I didn't want to risk it. I grabbed a set of barbeque tongs and slid open the glass door. The music was still playing, and I heard voices. I tiptoed toward the kitchen and caught a glimpse of Jules.

She caught me out of the corner of her eye and screamed. "Holy shit! Doc. You scared the hell out of me."

"Me? I thought you were a burglar. What are you doing here?"

"I didn't think you were home. The lights weren't on and I knocked."

"I was grading papers out back. I thought I heard something. You just let yourself in?"

"I still have a key." She flinched. "I'm sorry. We have a little surprise party planned for you and I thought I could sneak in and set up before you got back. I figured you were at the gym since it's Wednesday."

"I didn't renew my membership." I couldn't afford it anymore. "A surprise party? What for?"

"Well, it is the end of the semester. I'm graduating and won't be your teaching assistant anymore." She looked sad. "I wasn't sure whether I would see you this summer, so I decided to have a party."

"And you felt that the party should be at my place? Isn't there a place you kids have parties, like Chuck E. Cheese or something?"

"Trust me, Doc. You wouldn't have wanted to go to a party at my apartment. The toilet rarely flushes and it's tiny, tiny, tiny. Besides, the party is as much for you as for me."

"Okay, help me clean up a little. No underage drinking and everyone needs to clear out by eleven. It's finals week."

"Midnight?"

"Fine. But I'm serious about the drinking thing. I probably shouldn't socialize with my students, and I sure as hell don't want to get fired for it if there's an accident." The conservative me was shining through. I remembered my promise to Amy though, that I would lighten up. "Aside from that, let's get pissed."

"Yay!" Jules danced around as she loaded my dishwasher.

Within an hour there were probably forty people in my house. I worried about not having enough toilet paper for all the women. The good thing about a woman's college is that you don't have to deal with drunk fraternity boys. They allowed very few men in, and very few wanted to attend anyway because there were no sports teams. The bad thing is that there is never enough TP for all the girls, and there is always a line to the bathroom. I told Jules that people were welcome to use the master bath in the back of the house. She and Sarah agreed that strangers should use the guest bathroom. Apparently you never knew what people could do to your personal items. *The massive OCD of Jules and Sarah strikes again*—I was surprised they weren't handing out bottles of hand sanitizer.

I was overwhelmed by the number of well-wishers who came to the party. I talked to many seniors who had decided to pursue teaching and told me that I had a lot to do with that. I decided not to warn them about the negatives of the career and wished them well. There were also several alumnae present, former students who jumped at the chance to see me and tell me what they were doing with their lives. A lot of them were in grad school, some worked for publishing companies, and a few were even writers. I was awed by how many women had chosen language professions. I was a little jealous of their "freshness," just starting out with high hopes. Of course, I would not have traded my experience for anything in the world. At that party, I realized why I loved my job—because I loved sharing my passion for the English language with others.

I was also awed by the number of beautiful women who walked through my front door. I never really paid attention to appearance in class, mainly because most girls wore their comfy clothes. I will say that the girls cleaned up nicely, and there are some truly beautiful women in Texas. My mind raced to the most beautiful of all—Sam. I was wishing she was there to meet my students and hear their praises. On the other hand, I was glad she wasn't there or I would have been completely outed. I did have a fantasy that maybe Sam would show up. Maybe part of the surprise of the party was to have Sam make a grand entrance. After a month of not seeing her, I would risk being outed for the strong embrace of her arms. I guess subconsciously I was watching the door.

"Hey, who are you waiting for?" Sarah sat down next to me.

"Oh, no one. It's just my overactive imagination."

"Well, I know how much you miss her."

"What?" I assumed she meant Amy. Did she think I was waiting for Amy to show up?

"Sam. We can tell that you really miss her." Sarah seemed puzzled.

"Well, she'll be back next week." I was still hoping she was coming to the party.

"Yes. And in case you're watching the door hoping for a surprise, sorry. Jules called her and she has a final tomorrow afternoon. We did try to surprise you, but she honestly isn't coming to the party."

"Oh, I never thought she would come tonight." I swallowed my disappointment.

"Well, maybe you're watching the door hoping for the pizza guy?"

"Yeah, maybe I should call and see where he is. I'm starving," I lied.

"Hey, are you renting, or do you own this place?" Sarah whispered.

"Um. I own it." It seemed like an odd question.

"It's a great house." She looked around.

"It is. My brother and I put a lot of work into it. When I first moved in, it was a total shit hole. We redid the hardwoods, added the deck and knocked out a few walls."

"There's a rumor that you're going to move to Dallas when Sam graduates."

I couldn't admit that I spent all my money elsewhere, so I said, "We have looked a bit. But the search is on hold for a while." I was annoyed with her straightforward questions.

"Oh. That's too bad. I was hoping you'd be putting this place on the market." Sarah looked disappointed.

I had never really thought about the fact that I could sell the house. I kinda figured I would rent it out to some students. The location was perfect, midway between campus and area restaurants. Selling it could be an opportunity to regain some of the money I had used for Amy's bills. It might even be enough for half of a down payment, because surely by renovating the house I had increased its resale value. Plus I wouldn't have to worry about the headache of being a landlady. "Why, you lookin' to buy?"

"Yes." She blushed. "Jules and I have decided to move in

together."

"Wow, that was really fast. Even faster than most U-Haul lesbians. I'm impressed."

"I know. It just seems right. I'm sure you know what I mean."

"Well, Sam and I have never had an opportunity to live together. She's been off at school, and we travel nonstop during our vacation time. It's funny, I don't think we've ever had breakfast together that wasn't served by a waitress or room service."

"But if you could live together you would have done it a long time ago, right?"

"Yes, Sarah." I sighed. "I probably would have asked her to move in two days after we met."

"Well, if you decide to sell the house, let me know. Jules will be starting grad school here, so the location is perfect, especially since she hates to drive."

"I'll let you know. But I should tell you, these old houses are pretty expensive. I can't really afford to negotiate too much. Maybe, since you're both students, you should look over by South Point Park."

"I took a job at a cable company in Fort Worth. The commute is a bit long, but otherwise it's worth it. I think my new salary can cover a mortgage."

"So you dropped out of school?" I tried not to sound disapproving.

"Yes." She blushed. "It's a really good opportunity for me."

"Congratulations on the job, but please don't give up on school. I won't lecture you, but it's important to have an education to fall back on."

"I won't forget about school. Maybe I can take some night classes if the commute doesn't kill me. Oh, and you ended that last sentence with a preposition."

"At least you got more out of my class than a date with

Jules."

"I got a lot more. I got a lifetime with Jules." She smiled and started toward the kitchen.

"I love your optimism." I realized lately that there is no such thing as a lifetime.

Thursday was the last day of classes, the last day of finals. Part of me loved this day because it meant that summer was starting. Part of me hated it, because not only did I have to rush through a ton of paperwork, but I had to say good-bye to my students. This particular day, I was more stressed about the paperwork than I normally was, and I was pretty callous about the good-byes. A few students thanked me for the party, and I was glad to see that they weren't hung over. As each class began, I gave a little speech about how important it is to keep up with language skills and wished them all luck in their future. Then I handed out the tests and hid behind my desk to grade papers and work out averages. They would finish their tests, set them on my desk and file out one by one. I rarely looked up unless someone spoke to me, which probably gave students an easy opportunity to cheat. Fortunately, more than half of the test required an essay, so they couldn't cheat too much.

My three o'clock class was the last one of the day, and of the semester. I gave my little speech and handed out the tests. After about forty minutes passed, someone turned in a paper and spoke to me. "That was the hardest test I've taken all week. I hope I passed."

I didn't look up, but I immediately recognized the voice and smiled. "Well, I hope you passed too."

My beautiful Samantha stood in front of me wearing a baseball cap and a law school T-shirt. It was no wonder I didn't notice her before; she never wore a cap. I looked around the room and there were only five students left taking their test. In the back of the room sat Jules, who looked very proud if not elated.

"What are you doing here? Sarah said you had a final to take this afternoon."

"And I just took it, and it was a toughie. Are you going to grade it?"

"How about if I grade it tonight, naked, in bed?" I whispered.

"Okay, but if I pass, you have to do whatever I want. If I fail, I will do whatever you want."

"You got a deal. And by the way—" I waited as a student tuned in a paper. When she exited, I continued, "You look really adorable in your little college gear."

"Thanks, I thought it might bring a smile to you face."

All the students had left, and Jules was the only one left in the room other than Sam and me. Finally I climbed over the desk and jumped on her. I knocked her to the ground and kissed her sweetly scented neck. I had forgotten how much I loved her scent, her touch and her smile. It was the first time in a month that my smile felt genuine.

"Wow, happy to see me?" She put her hand on my face.

"Actually, I'm thrilled. This was a wonderful surprise. Are you done for the semester?"

"I am. I took my last test yesterday, but I had some things to take care of before I could come home. Jules told me about the party. I would have given anything to be there."

"No, this is a better surprise. I'll remember this forever, plus I get to see what you know about senior English." I kissed her hand.

We stood and stared at each other for a minute. Jules was still in the back of the room waiting for us. It was the first time I'd seen Sam since Amy died. That thought rushed into my head, and I guess it showed.

She put her hands on my shoulders and looked deep into my eyes. "Baby, how are you doing?" Her voice was soft and sincere.

"I'm fine." I bit my lip. "I'll be okay."

"You need to learn that the lip-biting thing really gives you away. We'll talk later, Dani."

Hearing the name Dani was like a slap in the face. I no longer felt like a "Dani" or a "Danielle"; those names belonged to Amy. I never wanted to hear them again. It was the weirdest reaction I had ever had to anything in my life, and it practically made me violent.

"Dani's dead. From now on, it's always Doc." I was breathing hard and my hands were shaking.

"Okay, I'm sorry. Doc it is. Anything you want, it's okay." She leaned in for a hug.

I flinched and moved back behind my desk. "I'm done here, shall we go?"

I could see Jules behind Sam looking uncomfortable and protective. In the rush of emotion, I must have become a little louder and angrier than I thought. They both stood there in front of me looking scared. It was the first time since Amy died that I felt any emotion that strong, and I wasn't sure what it was.

"Are you coming?" When neither one of them responded I said, "Fine, I'm going to Psycho's." I threw the tests in my bag and slammed the door shut behind me. Neither one of them followed.

"Was she like this all month?" Sam sat down, glancing nervously at the door.

Jules shook her head. "Quite the contrary. She's either been really quiet or really goofy. In fact, last week she spent an entire day telling jokes in all her classes. The students were in hysterics. It was one of the funniest things I've seen. Then the next day she was in a good mood but didn't want to talk. She made me give the lectures. We went out a few times and she seemed to really enjoy herself."

"How was she at the party last night?"

"She seemed fine. She didn't talk a lot. Sarah said she was watching the door for you all night."

"God, I hope she was watching for me." Sam sighed. "What do you think just happened here?"

"Actually, it's pretty simple. You know when a little kid falls off his bike, then just brushes himself off and gets back on." Jules came over and sat next to her.

"Yeah, then he rides off like nothing happened." Sam was seeing her point.

"Then the minute he gets home and sees his mom, or dad, or sister . . . suddenly the waterworks begin. It's not so much that he wants the attention as it is that he was scared but couldn't admit it till he got home. He had to be a big boy on the street." Jules glanced at the door like she wanted to leave.

"That could be it. Would make sense. There is another theory . . . maybe she's really angry and wants to lash out at someone. Maybe she knows she can take it out on me and I will forgive her." Sam stood, suddenly tired and ready for a drink.

"That's a good point. No one would yell at a friend, because a friend might not stick around. Maybe it's both. Maybe she's weak and angry. Maybe she's scared. Maybe Amy was the last person to call her Dani. But I would guess in about three hours she's gonna be giddy and possibly drunk."

"We'd better go to Psycho's." Sam held the door.

"And we'd better make it fun." Jules pulled out her cell phone to call Sarah.

Chapter Ten

I wasn't surprised to see the three of them walk into the bar. I was surprised to see them all wearing cardboard Burger King crowns. I peeled myself off the bar and moved to a booth near the dartboards. The three of them slid in on either side of me.

"What's with the crowns?" I asked, trying not to smile.

"Sarah was at Burger King when we called her. We grabbed some fries and stole about twenty crowns. Do you want one?" Jules pulled the folded cardboard from her purse.

"No, I'm good. I like the ball cap better." I tucked Sam's hair under her crown and mouthed "sorry."

"It wasn't as fitting for my princess lifestyle," she said then mouthed "it's okay" and winked.

"I graded your test."

"I thought we were going to save that for . . . um . . . later."

She smiled at Jules.

"Well, I was anxious to see if you've learned anything during my late-night lecture practices."

"And . . . how did I do?"

"You did really well on the multiple choice. Are you sure you kept your eyes on your own paper?" I pulled her test from my bag and unfolded it.

"Actually, my eyes were on you most of the time. How did I do on the essay?"

"Hmm. I'm not sure you understood some of the questions. See . . . right here where it asks for a comparison between these two epic poems?"

"Yes." She bit her nail.

"Your response was a comparison between Dixie Carter and Judith Light."

"Yeah. See, the problem is that I haven't read either of those epic poems since I was a junior." She shot me an innocent smile.

"Okay. But you misspelled three words and you referred to Dixie as 'smelly.' The word I was looking for was *stinky*."

"So, you're gonna take off points for that, Dr. O'Connor?"

"Don't call me that!" I shouted, then I started laughing. "I'm kidding. I swear."

"Oh, are you sure? It's important that we be Sybil to each other." She threw her crown at me and breathed what was clearly a sigh of relief.

"Sam, did Doc tell you our big news?" Sarah was beaming.

"I can't say that she has. Of course, we haven't had a chance to talk since Monday." I guess she didn't want it to seem that I didn't share their joy.

"Jules and I are moving in together." She took Jules's hand then looked furtively around the bar and dropped it.

"Wow, that's fast. Congratulations. I'm delighted for you."

She clinked her beer mug against Sarah's in a toast. "So you fell in love. Neither one of you has quirks so annoying that the other runs away to Africa?"

"We both have our idiosyncrasies, but the good thing is that we have the same ones." Jules winked at Sarah.

Sarah chimed in. "Yeah, like the fact that we're both a little bit anal."

"Well, Sam can be a little bit anal too." I started laughing and almost couldn't finish my sentence. "And I am not a fan of 'backdoor' sex, but I try to please her when I can."

Sarah and Jules totally missed the joke. Sam gave me the "right over their heads" hand gesture and laughed hysterically. "Oh, my gawd. You're such a jackass."

"Don't call me jackass!"

All four of us laughed on that one.

"So, did I pass my test?" Sam wiggled her eyebrows while I crawled into bed. "Or do I get to be your slave girl?"

"Actually, you did better than some of my students. But if you don't mind, I'd like to just lie next to you and talk for a bit." I was suddenly feeling a little lost and wanted to reestablish my emotional ties with Sam.

"That sounds great. Do you have a topic in mind?" She inched closer to me.

"I have a really light load this summer. How busy are you going to be interning?"

"Sorry to say, pretty busy. I stopped by the office earlier. The lawyers piled up my inbox in anticipation of my return to Dallas. Why? Was there something you wanted to do?"

"Nothing major. I hoped maybe we could slip off to Vegas."

"That's a definite possibility. Maybe a four-day weekend?" She smiled.

"Sure. And maybe we could put my house on the market."

"Really? You don't want to rent it out?"

"No. I think I could get enough equity out of this to make a down payment on a house in Dallas, despite my lack of savings."

"Hey, that's a great idea. So the search for our dream home is back on?"

"Probably. Actually, Sarah got some big job in Fort Worth, and she wants to buy this house for her and Jules."

"Think she could afford it?" She sat up. "Honestly, I doubt she'll be able to get a loan at her age. What is she, twenty-one?"

"Yeah. I thought that too. But if she starts her job this summer, maybe by fall she can prove on paper that she's capable. If we find a house, we might be able to move me in over Christmas vacation."

"Sounds like another definite possibility." She kissed my cheek. "I hate the fact that I'll be living out West when you move into our new home."

"It's okay. It will give me a chance to decorate the way I want without you and your mother picking out god-awful curtains."

"No decorating until I move in. It'll only be one more semester."

"Okay. Deal." I rolled onto my side. "Now, about that slave girl thing."

When I woke up Friday morning, Sam was already gone. She had to be in Dallas by eight to settle a few last-minute details for her internship. I was slightly hung over and regretted going out the night before. I had way too much work to do to be off playing with my friends. I loaded up some necessities and planned on staying on campus until the work was finished. When I got to my office, Jules and Sarah were there.

"We've graded all the multiple-choice parts; you just need to read the essay portions," Jules said.

"Oh, okay." I wasn't entirely comfortable with them doing my work for me. It was crucial that it be done with no mistakes since final averages were dependent on these tests. But it was my own fault for giving Jules my bag the night before.

"Don't worry. Sarah double-checked each one. We didn't make any errors."

"I trust you," I lied, secretly relieved they were conscientious.

"I've also done all the final averages for the tests you already graded earlier this week." Jules looked proud.

"Maybe I should double-check those." My flinch was surely obvious.

"It's not rocket science, Doc. You add up all the earlier grades and count the final as three grades, then divide by twelve." She held up a calculator.

I had to think about that for a second. I was using a slightly different method, which involved multiplying by a percentage. I did the math in my head, and sure enough her way was not only correct but a lot easier. I was kicking myself for using my long-drawn-out method all those previous years.

"That sounds right." It didn't matter much, I thought, if a student got a ninety-one or a ninety-eight in my class. It still showed up as a 4.0 on their transcripts. The final only really mattered for students who were borderline before the exam. "Did Sandy Brewer pass?"

"Her average came to fifty-nine point four—I thought you might want to decide whether to give her the D or the F. There are few on the verge that I left for you to decide." She handed me the stack of papers.

"How does that work, Doc? Do you have to go exactly by the numbers, or do you play a little favoritism?" Sarah asked.

"If they come to class, get the papers in on time and seem to really try, I'll give them the benefit and take the grade up. If they miss a lot of classes, or don't pay attention in class, I'll let the actual number stand."

"You don't take attendance, Doc," Jules pointed out.

I shrugged. "You can tell who's there. You get a feel for your classroom and get used to seeing a combination of faces. Like Sandy Brewer. She missed twice, and I never spoke to her, but she sat in the third row on the left. Jamie Sands must have missed twelve times. She sat in the back and actually slept through every lecture."

"You know everyone's name, even if you don't talk to them, don't take roll and don't have a seating chart?" Sarah seemed impressed.

"Yup. At first you label people in your head like 'girl with mullet,' 'girl with crutches' or 'gal with big feet.' Then when they turn in tests and assignments, you look at the name on the paper and match it to the label. Suddenly 'gal with big feet' becomes 'Jamie Big Feet Sands.' After the second assignment, I knew who everyone was by name. It takes years to get the memory thing down, but it's so much better than wasting time on introductions and seating charts."

Sarah laughed. "But there are lots of girls with mullets."

"So, you're saying that you know the names of all two hundred students that you have every semester?" Jules was clearly intrigued, and I suspected she was seeing herself in my shoes in years to come.

"I think so."

Jules must have accepted this as a challenge. "Okay. Monday at eight, second row, wears a sorority shirt every day."

"Annie 'Zeta' Sanchez." I smiled.

"Um, Tuesday at one, back row, blond hair."

"Olympia 'Sleepy Freshman' Miller." I was proud. "One more."

"Tuesday at two, big eyes, front row." Jules winked at Sarah.

"Sarah 'Stares at Jules a Lot' Mason." I winked at Sarah too.

"Is it true that some teachers are more lenient with attractive students than they are with homely ones?" Sarah was blushing.

"It may be true. There have been studies about that. I don't let appearances make a difference. That's my 'Butterfly Theory.'"

"What's that?" Sarah asked.

"Well, it never seemed fair to me that if a cricket, an ant, a roach or a spider came into your house that you'd kill it without thinking twice. But if a ladybug or a butterfly got in, then you'd open a door and help it outside with no injury. Do we decide which of nature's creatures gets to live because they're beautiful?"

"But crickets can ruin your fabrics, and roaches are dirty." Jules made a face.

"But do we have to kill them? Why can't we just lead them to safety just like we would a butterfly?"

"So you're saying that if you find a big hairy spider in your house that you open a door and lead it outside?" Jules laughed. "That could take hours."

"No, I'm saying that if I found a butterfly in my home that I'd squash it with a frying pan."

"Wow, the mind of a professor. I had no idea how much thought went into your profession." Sarah said sarcastically.

"Makes you want to stay in school, eh, Sarah?"

"No. But it's still fascinating." She laughed.

We managed to get all the paperwork turned in by three. I was delighted with their help and promised to cook for them one day in return. It was such a relief to have the classwork part done so I could concentrate on my departmental responsibilities. It was a lot of tedious things—mostly coordinating loose ends.

Unfortunately, no one could help me get that done. Sometimes I loved being head of the department; most of the time, I resented the paperwork and cursed the small difference in pay. I was dying to shirk it all and drive to Dallas. I wanted to spend the weekend at the Laine with my Laine. I sat at my desk lost in a daydream when a fleeting thought shot me out of my fantasy. Saturday was graduation. I was to speak at graduation. I had not written a speech. I was a huge putz and frantically dialed Sam's cell.

"Hey, dreamer. I'm a loser."

"Toby?" She laughed.

"Funny. How is your brother, anyway?"

"He's fine. He's off causing trouble in New Orleans this week. Why are you a loser?"

"Tomorrow's graduation."

"I know. I'll be there with bells on."

"I didn't write a speech."

"Oh, you're screwed. Can you get out of it?"

"Well, they printed the programs already. Unless you want to sit up all night and scratch my name off twenty-five thousand pieces of cardstock."

"Better brew some coffee, Doc. I'll meet you at the house at six."

I raced home, brewed some coffee and fed the cat. I thought about ordering a pizza but knew the food would just make me lazy. Sam showed up a little after six.

"How could I possibly forget something so important?" I whined.

"You've had a lot on your mind." Sam poured me a cup of coffee.

"How come no one reminded me?"

"Because no one thought you could possibly forget something

so important." She laughed.

"Bite me." I probably deserved that. "Do you think anyone would notice if I just recited some song lyrics?"

Sam rolled her eyes. "Depends on the song. If you did 'Mary Had a Little Lamb,' they might notice. If you did something a little more obscure you might be able to get away with it."

"Shit. I'm useless. I can't get up in front of that entire coliseum and recite lyrics." I poured some cream into the coffee mug and longed for a cigarette.

"How long does it have to be?"

"There's no time limit. I'm not the main speaker. I'm just representing the arts departments. I figure that I could get away with five minutes."

"Ah, that's nothing. I've heard you ramble on about the purpose of duct tape for longer than that. You can knock this out in no time."

"Okay, I'm going to sit on the patio and focus. You are way too distracting with your sarcasm and perky breasts."

"Fine. I will keep my breasts away from you until you're through. But I reserve the right to use my sarcasm if it becomes necessary."

I took my coffee outside and settled into a chaise lounge. Sam opened the living room window and sat down on the sofa. We were basically a foot apart, and with the window open I could practically hear her breathing. "Could you hold it down in there?"

"Write."

"Is that 'right,' like ten-four? Or is that 'write,' like with pen on paper?"

"I'm gonna kick your ass. Don't make me come out there."

"Right."

I stared at the moon and thought of so many things. My purpose was to give the graduates a little advice, a little motivation to conquer the world. As usual, I was giddy under stress. All I could think of were song lyrics.

I wrote down a few and tried them out on Sam. "How does this sound? 'You may find yourself, with a beautiful wife and a beautiful house.'"

"It sounds like the Talking Heads. What else you got?"

"'When you're alone and life is making you lonely you can always go downtown.'"

"Damn it, Doc. That's Petula Clark. You are a great leader and a great writer. Just think about what advice you needed when you graduated. Just tell them the truth about the world. They can hear song lyrics on the radio."

"Okay, but let me try out one more. 'Well East Coast girls are hip . . .'"

"I'm closing the window and locking the door. Knock when you have something inspiring."

I sat out there until three in the morning. A pot of coffee later, I had to pound on the window and wake up Sam to let me in.

"My gawd. Did you finally get something written?" She yawned.

"I think so."

"Can I hear it?" She got back on the sofa.

"You'll hear it tomorrow." I lay down on the sofa next to her and was asleep within minutes.

"I have been asked to speak here today because I have all the answers. I am going to give you all the advice you will ever need for the rest of your life. When you leave here today, you will have the knowledge you need to succeed. None of the classes you took over the last four years will prepare you for the world as much as what I am about to say. I hate to be the bearer of bad news, but the best years of your life are over."

I looked up and saw Sam shaking her head and smiling. She knew I wasn't going to take this seriously. I didn't want to disappoint her.

"Never again will you be able to sleep past noon. You must be in bed by ten p.m.—alone. You must wake up at six a.m.—alone. You will not be allowed to watch cartoons in your comfy bunny slippers anymore. You must now watch CNN wearing a starched shirt, pantyhose and high heels. You can no longer charge chips and beer to your father's gas card. You must now actually charge gasoline and coffee, and the bills will come to your house. You can no longer pick up strangers in a bar. You must now get drunk at your office Christmas party and pick up the guy from the mailroom . . . or the girl from the mailroom . . . it's your call."

I took a deep breath while waiting for the ripple of laughter to subside. "The most important thing to remember is that you make your own fate. You now have the opportunity to be as successful as you want, or as lazy as you want. You can take the skills you have acquired at this school and put them to good use. Or you can completely throw them away and become a carnival employee. The decision is yours. You will no longer be graded on performance; you will merely be fired if you don't perform well. You will no longer be given extensions or leniency; you will be given piles of work and no summer vacation. Basically what I am saying is . . . you are free."

I looked around at all the young faces and spotted several of my students. "Sometimes, as adults—yes, you are now really considered an adult. Sometimes, as adults, we take our freedom for granted. We take our lives too seriously. We work too hard and lose sight of what is important in life. As nice as it is to have a great career and lots of money, there are things we forget somewhere along the line. We forget what it's like to spend the entire day at a rock concert. We forget the thrill of finding a ten-dollar bill in our laundry and using it for an ice-cold pitcher of beer.

We forget the nostalgic smell of the old books in the beautiful campus library. And most important, we forget about the people who aided us on our path to adulthood. When you leave here today, take the time to embrace your friends. Tell them how much they've meant to you. It's likely that over the years, you will lose track of one another. These friends who made you laugh and made you cry will be a fond memory of days gone by. You will be so tied up in meetings and family life and traffic that you will never have friends this important again."

I glanced at my notes and was anxious to get the speech over with. "I was recently told that I needed to take life less seriously. I was told to lose my inhibitions and live a little. I was told to be free and happy. I can't tell you enough how important it is to heed that advice. Just do what makes you happy. Be free enough to enjoy your life. Let your parents do all the worrying for you while you take the time to dance . . . and love . . . and laugh . . . and live."

I received a polite round of applause. I think they were expecting more, something really profound. I didn't have anything profound to say. I just wanted to get through the darned speech so I could go home and have a drink and get some long overdue sleep.

"Now, it gives me great pleasure to announce the recipient of this year's Laine Scholarship Award. This award allows one student to continue her education at Central Woman's College. Basically, if she didn't already plan on going to grad school, she would have to go now. I am fortunate not only to have known her as a student, but she was also my teaching assistant this year. The Laine Scholarship Award goes to Jules Ritchie."

Sam shot me a look of surprise and I started laughing. She and I were the only ones who knew that the award didn't exist. I just knew that Jules was struggling, and being one of eight kids, she didn't want her father to worry. I'd decided that a little of the equity on my house, combined with a donation from the Laine trust fund, might be enough to help Jules go all the way. To spirited applause, I walked off the stage and sat down next to Sam.

"That was mighty last-minute," Sam whispered.

"Sorry I didn't ask you. I hope it's okay."

"No, it's fine. The family was actually considering starting a fund anyway."

"Good. Tell your family that they need to get a plaque made for Jules ASAP."

Chapter Eleven

Who doesn't love Vegas? The lights, the sounds, the depressing feeling of losing your entire paycheck on one hand of blackjack. We arrived around noon on a hot summer Wednesday in late May, and by six, I was down about . . . Let's just say I was a bit lighter in the pocket than I am in my loafers. I was never much of a gambler before, but somehow on this particular trip I was sucked into the excitement of the soft felt tables and shiny machines. I did manage to redeem myself a little around eight p.m. when I dumped a twenty into a slot machine and hit three chili peppers. The payout was $900, which meant that I wouldn't have to hit Sam up for a loan. Apparently ATM machines only pay out $400 a day.

After I cashed in my hefty load of dollar tokens, I went to find my partner in crime. She had planted herself at a high-dollar Caribbean Stud table, and I was thrilled to see a stack of chips in front of her. I pulled up the chair next to her, gave the dealer a couple hundred and pretended not to know Sam. She glanced my way but went along with the stranger charade. There were three greasy businessmen seated on the other side of Sam, I could tell they were getting on her nerves.

"You ready for a jackpot hand, little lady?" One of the greasy men spoke to me.

"Yes, sir, I sure am." I winked at him.

The dealer laid out the cards, and sure enough, I had a jackpot hand. I did my best to remain calm.

"How about that, sir. I do believe I have a jackpot hand here," I said to the dealer.

The greasy men started laughing and I saw the corner of Sam's mouth twitch.

"Better hope he qualifies, or you get next to nothing," another drunk man said.

The dealer did qualify and my four of a kind got me a mighty large payout. My first time at a high-dollar table and I was off to a great start.

"Beginner's luck," I said to everyone at the table as I tried to catch Sam's eye.

"Aw, she's not much of a talker. We've tried to get her to chat for an hour," the third drunk added.

"Is that right? Maybe she's concentrating on her game. Looks like she's the big winner at this table tonight." I gestured toward her chips.

"I'm just a little shy," Sam said in a girly voice.

I held back the obvious chuckle and considered the best way to play her game. "Well, you know, shy girls don't tend to bet two hundred dollars a hand." I set out a conservative fifty-dollar bet.

"You have to play big to win big." She placed five hundred dollars on the felt and waited for her cards. "What do you know, I believe I have a jackpot hand here, sir," she whispered to the dealer.

He finished the hand and qualified. He then turned to his pit boss. "The lady has a flush on a five-hundred-dollar bet here, boss."

I about fell out of my seat. "Lucky table for the ladies tonight." I laughed.

"You two must bring each other luck. A couple of Lady Lucks," one of the guys shouted.

Another drunken remark came from my left. "A payout like that deserves a big kiss."

"That's true," I said to the table. "Someone ought to kiss her."

The three guys looked at one another and the youngest got out of his chair and stumbled toward Sam.

"Shouldn't I get to choose who gets the kiss?" She laughed.

"Oh, sure." The guy sat back down and the three of them looked at her in anticipation.

Sam looked at the men and considered her options. Then she reached up, placed her arm around my neck and pulled my face toward hers. We kissed for a good minute and tried not to laugh at the hoots and hollers from the greasy group of men.

"Want to gamble some more, or do you want to get a room, Lady Luck?" she said loud enough for everyone to hear.

"Hmm. It *is* my lucky night. How about we gamble for another hour, then I will let you treat me to a suite and a bath. I'm Lucinda Smith." I held out my hand.

"Nice to meet you, Lucinda Smith. I'm Ophelia." She shook my hand and grinned.

"Ophelia what?" I had to ask.

"Ophelia later, you gorgeous vixen." She actually blushed.

The men stared at us with open mouths. None of them said anything the rest of the time we sat at the table.

❧

"You fared pretty well this evening," I said on the elevator heading to the room.

"As did you. Are you ahead for the day?"

I patted the wad of cash in my pocket. "I'm not just happy to see you. I think I got enough here to gamble a few days and still have plenty left to buy you a margarita."

"Okay, deal. Want to clean up and head over to Caesar's?"

"I was thinking maybe the Hard Rock, then we can grab a burger at their cute little diner."

She looked uncomfortable. "Um, I was thinking maybe save the Hard Rock till tomorrow. I'd actually prefer to stay on the strip tonight. We could get room service while we get dressed."

I didn't understand her reasoning, but I agreed. "So, really, how much are you up tonight?"

She started laughing, and just as the doors opened, she bolted toward the room. "If you want to see what's in my pocket, you're gonna have to catch me."

I chased her through the maze of hallways, into the room, and tackled her on the bed. All I found in her pocket was a receipt for cash totaling enough to buy a small condo on the beach. "Holy shit, Sammy. I think the margaritas are on you tonight."

"I think the Bellagio will be buying us a new car or two." She beamed.

I wasn't normally turned on by her wealth, but there was something sexy about the fact that she won this amount playing poker. I took the pile of cash from my pocket and threw it on the bed. Next, I pushed her down on top of the pile and we had giddy sex amidst a pile of crisp hundred-dollar bills. I should remark that this scenario should not be tried at home. Money does not smell great, it will stick to a sweaty body, and I am sure we lost a bit of the cash underneath the bed. The maid, I was sure, was thrilled.

❧

I awoke Thursday morning with a massive hickey on my stomach and a massive pounding in my head. We'd made it to Caesar's Wednesday night, and the Paris and the MGM. We danced at Club 54 at the MGM until the wee hours of the morning. Pretty much everything after two was a blur, but I did remember running into the three businessmen again, and I recalled giving them quite a show that surely led them to a Vegas prostitute or strip club. I looked around the room and realized that I was alone.

"Saaammmm?" I said too loudly, and my head practically exploded. No response. "Yoo-hoo, anyone home?" Again, there was no response. I crawled out of bed and tiptoed the forty miles to the bathroom. "Sam?" I whispered as I opened the door. I fully expected to see her passed out by the toilet, if she'd been as drunk as I was the night before. I looked everywhere in the large room, even the closets, and found no evidence of her presence.

I found a Red Bull in the fridge and some fresh bagels on the counter. After two bagels and three beverages, which included a Bloody Mary, I finally felt somewhat human. Still, there was no sign of my partner in crime. I took a long shower and as I stepped out of the tub, I was startled by a bellhop.

"Oh, my gawd!" I scrambled for a towel.

He stood and stared for an eternity before he finally said, "Um, Mrs. Laine asked me to bring up her items. I knocked several times and no one answered. I am really sorry." He blushed.

"It's okay. Maybe next time if you hear a shower, you might avoid the bathroom."

"I'm sorry. She told me to put this bag in the bathroom if no one was here. I guess she forgot some toiletries."

"Do you know where she is?"

"She's been downstairs using the computer and fax since eight. She said she'll be back to the room at one." He was still staring at me.

"Okay. Well, I can't really tip you right now." I gestured to my towel.

"It's been taken care of. And might I say, that's a hell of a hickey."

"Thank you. Please leave before I die of embarrassment." I was mortified.

Inside the bag was a bottle of perfume. I found two bags sitting on the bed. One bag contained two cowboy hats, and the other held two pairs of boots. I should say these were incredible vintage-style boots with red tips, the kind I'd wanted since I was a kid. Apparently work wasn't the only thing Sam had been doing since eight. I got dressed and watched TV. It took me a good hour to recover from the tragedy of a teenaged boy seeing my naval ring, tattoo and beet-red hickey.

We spent the afternoon playing dollar slots on Fremont Street. Just when I thought our luck had run out, I hit three sevens at the Golden Nugget. The fifteen hundred payout more than made up for the money we'd lost in the previous hours. I was woozy from the hangover and excitement. Sam seemed to be in great shape, which just reminded me of our difference in age. We had an early dinner/late lunch at New York New York and headed back to the hotel.

"You still want to go to the Hard Rock Casino tonight?" I asked, hoping for a calm night in the room.

"Yes, maybe around nine?"

"Okay, so perhaps this old lady could take a little nap?" I wanted to sleep for days.

"Nap away. I'm going downstairs. Maybe meet me at the roulette area around eight?"

"Okay. Put a little on number two for me."

"You got it." She kissed my head and headed out.

I lay in the room and stared at the ceiling for a while before I was finally able to drift off to sleep. I still had a strong feeling that something was missing, and no matter how hard I tried to distract myself, the feeling wouldn't evacuate my mind. I had a very intense dream during my three-hour nap, a dream of twos. Everything I saw was coupled. I dreamed of cats, two of them, I dreamed of mountains, two of them and I dreamed of me, two of me. When I awoke, I was overwhelmed by a sinking feeling in my stomach. The thought of two was too much for me: two hats, two pairs of boots, betting on the number two. I was a one, and the part of me that made me a pair was gone. I sat on the edge of the bed and cried.

It took me an hour to regain my composure enough to shower and dress. I put on my new boots and stylish straw hat, but I was still curious why she bought two of each. I assumed that one pair was for Sam, but the size was the same on both pairs, my size. I did my best with makeup to cover my puffy face, but it was still obvious that I had been crying. I decided to use a delayed hangover as an excuse, that or say I found a tear-jerker movie on cable.

A little before eight, I found Sam at a ten-dollar roulette table. She seemed to be having a great time but didn't have a lot of chips in front of her. I strolled up behind her and placed my arms on her shoulders.

"Boy, I hope that's Lady Luck behind me." She took her last stack of chips and placed it on the number two.

"I hope so too." I grimaced when I saw that she was still playing that same number. "How much in the stack?"

"It's around a hundred." She stood when the dealer spun the wheel. "Are you ready to go?" She pushed back her chair and took my hand.

Just as we started to walk away, the other players started shouting, "It's a two. Hey, lady, you won!"

We turned back around and saw the dealer stacking thirty-six hundred dollars in chips in Sam's place.

"That's incredible. We just can't lose." I beamed at her.

"Oh, to be honest, I started the table with four grand. That was the first time it hit."

"Sam, when I said play that number, I didn't mean exclusively."

"I know, but I love a challenge. I almost broke even here. Let's grab a cab and head to the Hard Rock."

We settled into a blackjack table at the trendy rock-and-roll casino. My mind wasn't really on the game, so I bet conservatively. Sam seemed a little distracted as well. I noticed she kept looking around between hands. All of the sudden, she grabbed her chips and announced that she had to go to the bathroom. I attempted to follow her, but she told me to keep my seat. I figured she was having an attack of the bad belly, so I allowed her some privacy.

About two hands later, a man took over her seat. I didn't look up at him, but he smelled really nice, a kind of familiar smell that reminded me of someplace I'd been.

Before I had a chance to look up at him, he said, "Stay very calm, Doc. No one wants to see you scream."

I immediately recognized the voice and did as I was told. "That seat is taken, you jackass." I almost started crying and couldn't remain calm any longer. "Holy shit, Jack! What on earth are you doing here?" I got out of my seat and wrapped my arms around my big brother's neck.

He chuckled. "I'm here to see Aerosmith. What are you doing here?"

"Aerosmith is playing here? I don't know whether I'm happier to see them or you."

"Yes, you moron, tonight in the Joint. Geez, read a paper once in a while."

"I take it that Sam got you out here." I gathered my chips and stood.

"Sam's here? Wow, what a coincidence." He motioned. "Let's go find her."

We walked around the casino looking for my partner, but with no luck. I checked all the high-dollar tables and didn't see Sam anywhere.

"Let's check the bar." Jack took my hand and led me to the corner area.

As we walked in, I immediately spotted Sam. When I looked a little closer, I noticed she was sitting with Sarah, Jules and a woman I didn't recognize. "Who's the blonde, Jack?" I elbowed his ribs.

"That's Sam. What? Are you high?"

"No, the taller one with the great jacket."

"That's Camille. She's one of my patients."

"Oh, are you rewarding her for flossing? Take all your patients to Vegas, do you?"

"No, just the ones I'm sleeping with." He blushed.

"Good for you. Sleep with your patients then take them across state lines. I'm glad I don't do that with my students."

"Um, aren't those two of your students sitting with Sammy?"

"Well, I never slept with them."

"The night's still young, and what happens in Vegas stays in Vegas, Dani."

My heart jumped and I felt faint. "Jack, could you call me Doc for now?" I grabbed onto his arm.

He made a motion to Sam that we'd be right back and escorted me outside. "What's going on, Doc? Are you okay?"

I immediately started crying and pushed my head onto his shoulder. "I just miss her so much. I try so hard to go on with my life, but I keep getting an eerie feeling like something is missing."

"I know. Shhh. It's okay." He stroked my hair. "That's why we're all here. Sam knows you're feeling lost and she wanted to give you a week away with fun and family."

"Oh, please tell me that Mom and Dad aren't here." I smiled.

"No, but Toby will be here in an hour or so with his floozy of the week."

"So it will be like a younger version of our parents." We laughed.

Jack said, "Look, I know how you feel. I get that lost feeling too, but I can't imagine it's as bad for me as it is for you. She was your twin and you have got to have that 'amputee' feeling. I'm not going to tell you to 'cowboy up' and get on with your life. You don't even have to take a big-girl pill. I'm not even going to tell you to try to have fun tonight. I'm just gonna say that we're all here to be with you. Sam is worried sick. She says you don't sleep, you rarely eat and you won't talk to her about it. She's afraid you're suicidal. Nothing in the world can replace Amy, and nothing will make the pain just disappear. But, Dan—um, Doc, it will get easier. You have to take better care of yourself because I can't lose another sister, not in my lifetime."

"Don't worry, Jack. I'm here for the duration. The only thing we have to worry about is the possibility of me running away with Steven Tyler."

"You *still* have a crush on him? It's been twenty years."

"And it'll be twenty more. Don't tell Sam. She thinks I'm gay."

"It's our little secret. Now come meet Camille. You're gonna like her a lot."

The concert was amazing; Sam scored us awesome seats. The highlight was seeing Camille throw her bra on stage, then watching Jack's face while she danced braless the rest of the night. He was right. I did like her a lot, not because of the bra thing, but because she knew how to make the most of a situation and have a good time. I was overwhelmed with a feeling of security, knowing that everyone took time to fly to Vegas for me. I know it wasn't a great burden to spend time gambling and seeing a concert, but it meant the world to me. For the first time since my sister died, I relaxed and had a good time. The best part of it all, I slept like a lamb and had happy dreams of rock stars and neon lights.

Chapter Twelve

The summer came and went in a blink of an eye. Sam had gone back to law school in California, and I was back at the university. We'd scoured Dallas high and low and never stumbled across our dream home. I got my house ready to put on the market . . . well, ready for Sarah and Jules to buy. We had arranged for them to close in October, thinking that Sam and I would have found a place by then. As October approached, I became a little panicky about being homeless. I knew I could stay at the hotel, but I dreaded the commute from Dallas. Sam pointed out that I would be making the commute anyway once we moved, but it seemed different to me, coming from a hotel rather than from a house every morning. It was important to me that I felt settled and secure. The anxiety of displacement grew with each box I packed. Finally, with two weeks until the deadline, a phone call from my brother brought the solution to my problems.

He started talking before I finished saying hello. "Hey, Doc, I've got great news."

"I could use some good news. Or a good newspaper with a decent real estate page."

"Camille's grandmother passed away last week."

"Wow, Jack," I said dryly. "That is great news. What else makes you happy? Did her cat get run over, or did someone steal her car?"

"Okay, that was rather callous. I am sorry for her loss. But the good part of it is the house."

"There's a house? Okay, I think I see where you are going with this. Continue."

"Her grandparents have lived in this bungalow in Lakewood since the Forties. It's an amazing house in really good condition. Her grandfather was a carpenter, so everything is in great working condition—good plumbing, wiring, even a solid foundation."

"Lakewood, eh? That's one of my favorite parts of Dallas. What's the situation on ownership?"

"Her grandfather is still living there, but he wants to sell it . . . too many memories. He wants to move to Florida anyway. I think he has a lot of friends out there."

"How big is it? What about the price range?"

"Well, it's a little higher than you'd like, but it's totally worth it. Maybe about twenty grand more than your budget. It's got three bedrooms, two baths, a pool, office, two living areas, detached garage and amazing back deck."

"What about the neighborhood. Are we talking good Lakewood or desperately in need of attention Lakewood?"

"Doc, it's beautiful. You don't think I'd let my girls live in the 'hood, do you?"

"Is he going to list it?"

"He is, but I asked him to hold off. He'd rather not deal with a realtor if he doesn't have to. This could be a solution for both you and him. Want to come see it?"

"Sure. When?" I couldn't wait to call Sam.

"Pack a bag, let's do the Friday night bowling thing and we can go see it in the morning."

"Okay. Can I stay with you? The hotel is so depressing when Sam's away."

"Um, you're welcome to stay. Camille will be here though."

"Just tell her to keep her bra on and the noise down."

"Meet us at the Attic at seven. It's closer to my office and I don't want to drive home and go back out."

"Okay. Get back to work. Surely there's a patient waiting to be tortured."

"It's so great to be paid to be a sadist. See you at seven."

I was so relieved at the possibilities that I was practically dancing. I checked my watch and decided to catch Sam between classes.

I began my rant before she finished saying hello. "Sam, you're not going to believe this but Jack called and Camille's grandmother died and they're selling the house and it's exactly what we're looking for." I spoke so quickly that the words were slurred together.

"Okay. Now take a breath and repeat that in English. All I got was something about Jack and Camille."

"Argh. Jack called and Camille's grandmother died."

"Oh, my. We should send some flowers."

"Yes, I will. But that's not the good news." I remembered how callous Jack had sounded.

"Well, I should hope not," she said sardonically.

"Her grandparents have a bungalow in Lakewood and it's going up for sale." I was surprised to hear so much joy in my own voice.

"Oh. Nice area. You know there are a lot of problems with

those old houses, Doc." She was raining on my parade.

I explained, "He was a carpenter. Jack says it's in mint condition. I'm going to Dallas tonight and we're going to see it tomorrow."

"Well, I hope it's a good one. I'll keep my fingers crossed." She sounded bitter.

"Is something wrong?" I picked up on her attitude.

"No, I was just hoping we'd stumble across something together. I am a bit jealous that you get to see the house with Jack and Camille."

"Well, don't guess you can fly in tonight?"

"No, baby, I've got stuff to do." She sighed.

I knew that by stuff she meant she had plans with friends. We had a deal that we could maintain active social lives in separate states as long as our clothes stayed on. "Football game tomorrow?"

"Yes, and a big party tonight with the other legal types."

"Okay. Well, I promise not to make a decision until you've seen it. If it looks like a keeper, maybe you can come see it next weekend?"

"That I can do, Doc. I've got to run. Call me later."

She hung up before I had a chance to say anything. I was a little pissed that she chose a party and football game over house-hunting. Of course, I sometimes forget that not everyone has the luxury of flying state-to-state at the drop of a hat. If she wasn't a Laine, she could never afford to hop a plane on an hour's notice. I decided to forgive her for wanting to enjoy her law school experience. I threw a duffle bag in the car and headed to Dallas.

Camille's grandfather, Rob, was in his eighties, and he acted accordingly. When we got to the house, he met us on the porch. I swear it took us twenty minutes to finally get into the house. This annoyed me to no end, given my anxiety. I loved the outside, the landscaping and even the quaint little duck-and-goose mailbox. The entryway had an arched door that led to the living room, and there were amazing original hardwood floors throughout. The walls could use some paint, but I was delighted to see that there was no paneling. The master bath boasted a huge shower with dual showerheads and a cute claw foot tub. The kitchen definitely needed some upgrading, but the island counter and SubZero fridge were definite selling points. I instantly fell in love with the backyard, with its lap pool, honeysuckle bushes and overgrown hibiscus. The den had plenty of room to transform it into the ultimate media room, and the guestrooms were plenty big. The best feature of the house, other than the built-in book-shelves in the office, was the master bedroom fireplace. I decided then and there that, like Camille's grandparents, I could grow old in that house. There was no doubt in my mind that I had just stumbled across my future home, and I knew it wouldn't take much to convince Sam of the same.

Like Jack told me, it was a bit out of my comfort zone price-wise. Despite the fact that Sam could afford to pay cash, we had a deal that it had to be affordable enough for me to pay half the down payment and half the mortgage. The house was really a lot larger than we needed, by about fifteen hundred square feet. I dreaded cleaning such a monstrosity, but I had to remind myself that it was indeed love at first sight. I'd had the feeling of instant love once before in my life, and it had proven to be the best thing that ever happened to me. I knew I could stretch my budget enough to make another decision work. I couldn't help myself, I told Grandpa Rob that I'd take it. I didn't even consult Sam or give her a chance to see it. I just knew that it was my home, and I wanted it as soon as possible.

I dreaded making the phone call to Sam. We'd had a few fights in the past, and all of them were about problems with the long-distance thing; this was no exception because I made a life decision without her. I hoped she would understand, but I knew that if I was in her place, I would be pissed about a commitment to a house I'd never even seen.

I got back to my house, took a Vicodin for some unknown reason and picked up the phone.

"Sammy! How's life on the West Coast?"

"It's okay, baby. How was the house?"

"It's amazing. I have never felt so at home in my life." I cringed, waiting for her response.

"That's great. I'm coming in on Thursday night. Can we see it Friday?"

"Um, Sam . . . I committed to buy it." I cringed again, ready for a fight.

She was silent for a minute. "Will the kitty like it?"

"He can have his own room. You will love it, I promise."

"As long as you'll be happy, then I'll be happy."

I was astounded by her response. I fully expected bitterness. "Are you sure? Are you still gonna come and see it?"

"I'm sure. I'm thrilled you are doing what you want." The tone in her voice told me that something was up.

"Okay. Spill it."

"Spill what?"

"You're being too calm. I know you can't survive in a place that doesn't meet your personal criteria." I was still waiting for the fight.

"Doc, I know you wouldn't put us in a place that didn't make me comfortable."

"True. And?"

"And . . . I made out with a freshman last night."

My stomach sank and I wanted to vomit. "Please tell me it meant nothing."

"It meant nothing. I know our rule about clothes staying in-

tact. We've both kissed others in the last year. I just felt I should
tell you."

I knew she wouldn't have made a point to tell me so formally
if it wasn't a big deal to her. "Sam, should I worry?"

She hesitated. "No . . . of course not."

Somewhere between the Vicodin, the disrespect for the plans
I was making for our life together and the fact that she hesitated,
I was furious. It may have been jealousy, it may have been disap-
pointment, or it may have been the fact that I couldn't take losing
another woman in my life. I simply said, "Fuck you, Sam." Then
I slammed the phone down so hard that I cracked the cradle.

I thought about calling Jack and telling him that the house
deal was off. I thought about calling Jules and asking her to take
me to the nearest gay bar so I could prey on a freshman myself.
Instead, I took two more Vicodin and slipped into bed. There was
nothing in the world that I could do to make the pain go away.
As I drifted off to sleep, all I could think about was Amy. If she
were still alive, I would have called her and let her tell me a story
of our youth. I would have laughed and realized that the world
was full of giggles and memories. I was angry that I couldn't call
Amy. I was angry that Sam was so many years younger than I
that a freshman would seem glorious in comparison to me. I lay
in bed wishing that I was straight, that I was younger and that I
was stronger.

I don't remember falling asleep, and I don't remember waking
up sick as a dog before dawn. The only reason I know that I did is
because I had brought in the paper and written myself a reminder
to cancel the delivery service. I know that I took the last several
Vicodin, because I found the empty bottle the next day. I know
that I was angry because I found a broken plate in the kitchen.
Apparently I was injured from the plate because I found a trail of
bloody paper towels throughout the house. It was around noon
before I was capable of moving. I dragged myself to the shower

and searched my body for cuts. I found a minor gash on my left
arm that would require a big bandage but no stitches.

I was extremely groggy, but surprisingly, I felt pretty good,
considering the number of painkillers I'd ingested. I was definitely not feeling any pain, not even any type of hangover side
effects. I went back over my last conversation with Sam. I wasn't
as upset in the daylight as I had been the night before. I tried to
analyze what it was that upset me enough to kill off an old bottle
of medication. I decided that it was the thought of change, of
losing Amy, of moving to the city, and then the insecurity of Sam
indulging in a younger, sexier woman. She was right in telling
me what happened, and normally I wouldn't have been bothered.
I think it was the tone in her voice that pissed me off. She had
sounded very serious, unlike in the past when she told me like it
was some big drunken joke. I knew that we had very casual rules,
and I also knew that she'd never look at another woman the way
she looked at me. I decided that it was time to take Jack's "big-
girl pill" and start accepting the changes in my life. The pills I
took the night before were definitely not going to help, but I sure
came damn close to breaking my promise to Jack that I was here
for the duration.

I went to the kitchen to call Sam. I saw by the caller ID that
she had phoned again last night. I checked the answering machine and realized that I must have been pretty well passed out.
I had seven messages and hadn't heard the phone ring once. I
patiently waited as each message played.

"Doc, please don't be mad at me. I promise it meant nothing,
and I am so sorry I ruined your good news about the house.
Please call me back, anytime."

Beep.

"Doc, it's me again. Are you home? I tried your cell. Just call
me. I love you."

Beep.

"Doc, it's midnight in Texas. I know you don't have to work tomorrow, but you're never out this late. I'm getting worried. Please call me."

Beep

"Okay, I fucked up. I know you don't care if I have a drunken kiss. I shouldn't have brought it up when we were planning something as important as the house. You know you're my whole world. Well, I hope you know that. I wish I could come home." She sighed. "I miss you so much, and that's no reason for me to kiss someone else. I am a total jackass, and I will do anything to make you feel better. I know you're going through so much right now, and I'm so sorry that I'm not there to be with you. You should be the one out having fun and kissing freshmen. Oh, well, maybe as a professor you shouldn't kiss students. I know you don't feel close to me, and I'm probably not making things any easier fo—"

The machine cut her off.

"Doc, it's Jules. Sam was looking for you. I called earlier and the phone just rang and rang. I know it's really late, and I hope I didn't wake you. Sarah drove by your house and saw your car, so we'll just tell Sam you must be sleeping. Call me tomorrow. Maybe we can do dinner?"

Beep.

"Hey, baby. I called Jules earlier, and she called me and said you were home, maybe asleep. I know you'd pick up the phone if you were there. Gosh, I hope you're not trapped under a heavy object or stuck in the shower because of that broken door. I'm going to bed now, but call if you get this message. I love you, and I'd like to leave you with this little poem I wrote: Please don't be mad/I want you to be glad/that we found a home/and I'll buy you a gnome/and neither of us will roam/and I need some sleep/sorry I'm a creep/and here comes the beep."

Beep.

"Good morning. It's me, the poet. You're probably at the weekly brunch. I miss the Sunday brunches with the butches. I'm off to church—yes, my aunt is insisting. I'll call you later."

I felt pretty stupid after hearing her messages. She probably thought I was screening them, and I didn't want to confess that I'd drugged myself and couldn't hear the phone. It was too late to go to the Butch Brunch, and I wasn't hungry anyway. It occurred to me that I hadn't eaten anything substantial in quite some time, so I called Jules and made dinner plans. I settled into the Sunday crossword and waited for Sam to call back. I didn't want to interrupt during her time with her aunt. I was totally brain dead and couldn't fill in a single answer on the puzzle. I figured it would be fruitless to make an attempt at grading papers. I stared at the wall and daydreamed about the way things were two years ago when Sam still lived in Texas, before Amy got sick. I would have given anything to go back to that time. I must have sat there and daydreamed for an hour before the phone broke the silence.

It was Sam. "Doc, thank Peter. Are you okay? I was so worried that I almost jumped a plane."

"I'm fine. Stay where you are."

"Are we good? I am so sor—"

I cut her off. "You don't need to apologize. I'm sorry I hung up on you. You can kiss all the freshmen you want. I totally trust you, and you don't even need to tell me."

"Baby, the only reason I hesitated is because I wasn't sure whether I should confess that it was a boy and not a girl that I kissed." She laughed.

"Oh. Well, are you still playing on the girl's team?" I was honestly worried.

"Oh, more than ever. I think it was a curiosity thing. He's some studly brother of one of my friends. He's very cute and dumber than a bag of golf balls. I couldn't resist. I don't know why."

"Well, you haven't been with a lot of people, so maybe you wanted to see what the straight kiss was like. I'm glad you didn't run out and become a Republican and buy a minivan with this guy."

"No, the only thing I'm doing is buying a house with you. You still want to live with me?" she asked.

"I'm just having a lot of trouble with everything going on in my life. I'm making a lot of changes in my life. I'm building my world around you."

"You're not going to burst into a Dixie Chicks song, are you?"

"Fleetwood Mac," I corrected.

"Who?" She sounded serious.

"Oh, dear. See, there is a bit of an age difference here."

"Oh, don't worry, Doc. I swear I'm kidding. I'm quite familiar with Mick, Lindsey, Stevie and Christie."

"You are? Whew." I was actually relieved.

"Of course I am. My parents saw them in concert a few times."

"Argh. Just when I think you've redeemed yourself, you suck me back into the gap."

"Seriously, I don't even notice the age difference. I'm mature for my age. I grew up fast, remember? You're the one I want, wrinkles, gray hair and all."

"I'm in this for the long haul, Sammy. If you think you'll ever have second thoughts, I need to know now."

"I'm in this game of chance with you—no second thoughts, no more kissing freshmen. I'll be there this week, and we will buy that bungalow. But I expect you to tell me the difference between a house and a bungalow before we sign the papers."

"The difference is about twenty grand." I flinched.

"Is that stressing you out?"

"A little."

"It'll be okay. We'll figure it all out and live happily ever after."

"Yay." I couldn't think of anything else to say, but I had my fingers crossed for luck. "I have to go in a bit. I'm meeting the newbies for dinner. But I want you to know that if the opportunity arises, I still reserve the right to kiss a stranger."

"As long as you remember to tell me all about it, and kiss me more."

"It's a deal," I promised. "I'm sorry I didn't answer the phone all night. I was sleeping hard."

"I think I understand." She sounded as though she knew my secret. "Just relax, and know that everything will be okay. I adore you, dreamer."

"Okay. I adore you too. See you in a few days."

Chapter Thirteen

I picked Sam up at the airport on Thursday night. We went straight to the gay bars and managed to be shitty drunk by eleven. I had the foresight to call my new TA and ask her to take my Friday classes. We were scheduled to see Rob's house at nine on Friday morning. There was a bit of awkwardness between us, and I have no explanation why. We acted more like old school chums than partners. We didn't have any physical contact all night, our conversations were strictly intellectual and flirtation seemed to be a foreign concept. After a few shots, we decided to play our little word game that had gotten us through so many nights at the bars. The game was simple. One of us came up with a word or phrase, and the other one had ten minutes to chat with a stranger and use that word or phrase in a conversation. It had to be a legitimate sentence, and it couldn't merely be shouted out like a Tourette's incident. We flipped a coin to see who would go first. I won. The stakes were high. If I didn't complete the challenge, I had to do karaoke on Friday night. I was up to the challenge, and my word was *tiddlywinks*. The clock started as soon as I repeated the word and got confirmation. I immediately scoured the bar, looking for my victim. I located a nice butch with a mullet and made a beeline for her. Sam stood behind me, close enough to listen in.

"Hi, I'm Lucinda." I held out my hand.

She gave me a distrusting smile. "I'm Marsha." The handshake was not returned. "Don't try to pick me up. My wife is in the bathroom."

"Oh, I wasn't going to pick you up. I just thought you had a familiar face, so I thought I'd say hello and be friendly." I knew it was hopeless. Of all the women in the bar, I picked the one with no sense of community.

"Look, unless you want your ass kicked, I suggest you move along."

"Okay, no harm, no foul. I'm with my mate." I gestured toward Sam. "We just thought maybe you guys would like to play a game of tiddl—"

"Give it up. We aren't into couples," she interrupted.

"Okay, well I'm sorry to hear that. We really thought you were a sexy couple. Our loss." I walked away.

Sam was laughing her ass off. "A sexy couple? You know that word is gonna get around that we're on the prowl for a foursome."

"I know. Maybe we should make this quick. If you score, I do karaoke. If you fail, we're tied and the game carries over."

"Got it. What's my challenge?"

"The password is *upsy-daisy*," I whispered in my best emcee voice.

Sam confirmed the word and looked around the room. When

she had her target in sight, she led me forward. As we approached a table of women, Sam stuck her leg out and tripped me. I fell halfway to the ground and she grabbed my arm and pulled me back up. The girls at the table took notice of the incident. Sam looked at the table and made a motion to them that I was drunk.

"Oh, looks like you guys have had enough," one of the women said.

"Hell, she does it all the time. I just stay behind her and if she falls, it's like, upsy-daisy, and I help her back up again." Sam grinned.

"Well, maybe you shouldn't trip her," another woman added.

"What's the fun in that?" Sam took my hand and led me to the back patio.

"You ass! That's dirty pool, you can't trip me to get the word in!"

"Whatever it takes to win, lady. Better let Jack and Jules know that you'll be singing at the Attic tomorrow night. Maybe a record producer will discover you and you can be famous. You could name your first album *Upsy-Daisy*."

"All right. I concede. You win. You're buying breakfast." We headed to the café across the street.

Friday morning came too soon. I hit the snooze button for an hour and it was after nine by the time we got to the bungalow. I could tell by the look on Sam's face that she was in love with the place before we even stepped inside. Rob was welcoming with coffee and doughnuts, which were perfect for a hangover situation. We took a tour of the house, and he was a bit more descriptive this time than he was when I first saw the place. He told us how to work the pool, who to call if there were problems, and he even described the neighbors. I think he had a crush on the old lady next door, but he was the type who'd never admit it since he was recently widowed.

Sam asked to use the bathroom. He told her, "My house is your house." Then, after she went into the room, he shouted through the door, "Oh, that toilet needs a little repair. We follow the golden rule on that one."

"Um, what's the golden rule, Rob?" Sam called.

"You know. If it's yellow, let it mellow. If it's brown, flush it down."

"Um, okay. Thanks."

Rob and I stood in the kitchen for a few minutes before I heard the toilet flush. I couldn't help but to giggle.

Sam reappeared shortly thereafter. "All right, I realize that I flushed it down. I'm hung over as a Mother Hubbard, so what do you expect? Okay, Rob, we'd better take the house since I've already marked my territory."

"Well, there you go. One minute you're homeless, next minute you flush and have to write a check." I laughed.

And there it was. We made a major purchase together and it was the first day of the rest of our lives. Of course the need to celebrate got the best of us. We met Jack, Camille, Jules, Sarah and several other friends at the Attic. The main attraction was to be me in the act of paying off a bet. Karaoke started at ten, and we arrived at eight. I drank as many draft beers as humanly possible in those two hours and still wasn't drunk enough to force myself on stage. I pored through the list of songs and couldn't find anything I recognized. Sam made a few suggestions of smoky love songs, but I couldn't make myself sing a love song in front of my brother. I knew I should sing something that Sam would love, but my heart kept telling me what it had to be, and it was for Jack. The deejay introduced me and I did the best I could.

"We get it on most every night. When that moon is big and bright, it's a supernatural delight, everybody is dancing in the moonlight . . ." I got lost in the song and tears never occurred to me.

By the time I finished, I was so involved that I could have sung all night. After a solid round of applause, I took my seat. Sam hugged me and said she was impressed. She didn't know the significance of the song, and I looked around for my big brother.

"Camille, where's Jack?" I asked.

She looked around. "I think he ran to the car."

I went outside and found him smoking by the entrance. "Jack, you don't smoke." I took the cigarette away from him and took a puff.

"That was without a doubt the most surreal moment of my life." He stared at the ground.

The word *surreal* resonated in my head. Amy had said it so many times the day she passed. "I'm sorry. It's such a great song, and I thought it would be good for both of us to hear it again."

"It was great to hear it. I'm glad you sang it, but I was just caught off guard a little. Every time I think I'm okay, something reminds me of . . . well, I just feel sad all over again."

"I know what you mean. I'll be driving along, then I'll see a car like hers, and even though she never lived here, I look to see if it's her. When I realize it's not, a wave comes over me and I realize I will never see her again. It seems like it takes me days to recover from things like that sometimes. I'm sorry I made you sad tonight. This was supposed to be a celebration. We're finally gonna live in the same city."

"That is cause for celebration. I'm thrilled that you and Sam have found a place to plant your feet and sit still for a while. You two are the perfect couple."

"And . . . what about you and Camille? Are you following Amy's orders and settling down and having a son anytime soon?"

"Honestly, I don't think she and I have what it takes. She kinda gets on my nerves, and we have nothing in common. She doesn't even like *Rocky Horror*."

"Doesn't like *Rocky Horror*?! You have to dump her immediately. She'll never let you dress up as the Sweet Transvestite on Halloween. Seeing you in garters is the highlight of my year."

"Who would have thought that I would own more fishnet stockings than my own sister."

"It's okay. I probably own more flannel shirts than you. It all balances out. So let's go inside. I'll sit next to the woman of my dreams and you can sit next to your future ex-girlfriend."

"Okay." He opened the door. "Hey, kiddo, you can call me when you're sad. Maybe we can recover faster if we do it together."

"Maybe so. You can call me too." I kissed his cheek.

Sarah and Jules made it home a little after two. Jules was the designated driver, and Sarah was three sheets to the wind. It took twenty minutes to get Sarah up the flight of steps to Jules's apartment. She sat down about every third step and recited the alphabet, just in case there was a test later. She claimed that she couldn't be that drunk if she could remember her ABCs. Jules did not find any humor in the situation and was growing annoyed with her inebriated girlfriend. She thought she would get Sarah undressed and in bed before the next wave of nausea set in, but she wasn't so lucky. Sarah threw up on the sofa, the coffee table and Jules's shoes.

"Wow, I've never seen you puke before. It's quite a sight." Jules was dabbing paper towels on her sandals.

"You've never seen me drunk before. There're lots of things

you've never seen me do. Did you know that I can play the violin? Did you know that I'm an awesome chess player?"

"Wow, you must have been really popular in high school." Jules had a mental image of Sarah being the biggest nerd in her class.

"Hey! Just because I'm smarter than you doesn't mean you can make fun of me."

"Smarter than me? You assume you're smarter because you can play chess?"

"I'm smart enough to have a high-paying job at the age of twenty-one. You're older than I am and you're still in college." She wiped the vomit from her shirt.

"Okay, Drunky McDrunk. You need to go to bed." Jules feared that their first fight was brewing.

"What? You know I'm right, huh? You don't want to talk about it because you know you're not as smart as me."

"As smart as *I*," Jules corrected.

"Oh, what the fuck ever. You wouldn't know shit if you didn't work for Dr. O'Connor last year. You never would have gotten that scholarship if it wasn't for Sam and her money."

"Okay, Sarah. I am aware that the scholarship was a gift among friends, but I am smart enough to take advantage of the offer and use it to get the education I need to further my career. What happens if you get fired? You won't have your education to fall back on. You'll lose your new car and you won't be able to buy Doc's house."

"I won't get fired. They need me there and I'm very good at my job. Plus, if we need money, we can just call Sam and she'll help us."

"I'm sure you're great at your job, but things happen. You can't guarantee anything in life. And I would never ask Sam for money."

"You already took her money for school. What difference

would it make?"

"It makes a huge difference. Look at Doc. She could quit her job and live off Sam's money, but she has pride. She insists on paying her own way, and I know for a fact that she doesn't take a dime from Sam. I admire her for that, and I have my pride as well."

"Things happen, huh? You can't guarantee anything in life? What are you trying to say? Maybe we weren't meant to be together? Maybe we won't last?"

"No, that's not what I'm saying. I can't predict the future. All we can do is try and hope that it works out." Jules was growing angry.

"Yeah. I need to go to bed." Sarah acted as though it finally occurred to her that she said awful things in her drunkenness.

"Ya think?" Jules escorted her to the bedroom and watched her collapse on the bed.

Jules was obviously upset. I could tell the minute I answered the phone.

"Hello?" I whispered, hoping that Sam wasn't awakened by the ringing.

"Doc, it's Jules. I'm sorry to call so late."

"It's okay. Are you guys all right? You were okay to drive, weren't you?"

"Oh, I was fine. We got home fine. Sarah's the drunk one." Jules let out a long sigh.

"We had a fight."

"Ah, I take it this is the first fight of your perfect and exciting relationship?" I tried to sound serious but couldn't help but smile at the idea.

"Yes. I don't know if it was a bad fight. I don't know if she meant everything she said."

"Well, she probably won't even remember everything she said. Some people are more honest when they're drunk, some are full of shit. You won't know until tomorrow what type of drinker she is." I was still trying to be serious.

Jules asked, "Do you remember the first fight you had with Sam?"

"Vaguely. We were both drunk. In fact, I can't. I think ninety percent of our fights happened when one or both of us was beyond tipsy. We've said some terrible things to each other, some things we meant, some we didn't. Things just build up, and once in a while, it's good to let them out." My mind raced through some previous cat fights and I couldn't help but laugh out loud.

"Do you forget about it the next day?" She sounded anxious.

"Sometimes. I've stormed out a time or two. She's left many times. It can be awkward the next day, but you just get over it. You have to. You may not forgive, or forget, but you have to remember that you, like Sam and me, are two strong-willed women. There is no way that two women can live together without each thinking that one of them is right and the other is wrong."

"So you think we'll fight like this again?"

"Oh, hell, I'm willing to bet that you'll have worse fights than this. The key is to learn to pick your battles, and try not to bring up things when you're drunk. Maybe let them out a little at a time and don't let things fester. You may be madly in love with her eighty-five percent of the time, and that other fifteen percent . . . well, she may drive you nuts. But as long as the good always outweighs the bad, then you should be okay."

"I hope you're right."

"What was the fight about anyway? If you don't mind my asking."

"She said she's smarter than me."

"Smarter than *I*," I corrected.

"See! That's what I said. I corrected her and she got even more pissed. She thinks that because she got a great job and can play chess that she's smarter . . . I'm just a college student."

"If I had to guess, Jules, I'd think she's just trying to make herself feel better about leaving school to take the job. Maybe she is a bit jealous that you're going to be a professor and she'll be stuck in her first job forever."

"I hadn't thought of that. Still, that's no reason to make me feel stupid."

"No, it's not, but when you've had eight beers, do you ever follow the course of logic?"

"Ah. I guess that my little Sarah is not a mean drunk, but an insecure drunk."

"It's possible. My advice? If that proves to be the case, be damn sure you don't flirt with anyone when she's drunk. If she gets insecure then she'll get jealous."

"Thanks, Doc. Sorry I woke you. Are you sure you don't remember what your first fight was about?"

"Let me think. I don't remember. Oh, hang on. Sam's up." I covered the phone and asked if she remembered what out first fight was. She knew immediately and I was almost embarrassed to tell Jules. "Okay, our first fight was about a month after we started dating. We got shitty drunk at a campus function, and when we got back to my house she let my cat out. I accused her of hating Kitty and she accused me of liking the cat more than I liked her. We yelled for an hour and slept in separate rooms. The next morning she brought the cat into my room and we all had breakfast in bed."

"Damn, that's a pretty stupid fight. I hope we can have breakfast together tomorrow."

"I hope so too. Just get some sleep, don't worry about it and above all, don't try to wake her up to talk."

"Thanks. Tell Sam I'm sorry I woke ya'll."

"Good luck, call us tomorrow."

I hung up the phone and rolled over to face Sam, who was smiling.

"What are you so happy about?" I stroked her hair.

"You're here with me at the hotel." She laughed.

"Yes, I am. Thanks for noticing."

"What I mean is that you're here with me in Dallas, and that damn cat is all alone tonight sixty miles away. It's obvious that you like me more."

"Actually, I spend more nights with the cat than I do with you. Maybe you ought to rethink the math on that one." I settled myself on her pillow and closed my eyes.

"Damn it, Doc. I never thought of it that way. Now I'm gonna be up all night worrying about that."

"Go to sleep, dork. I love you more. Are you happy?"

"Yes, I'm happy. But I can tell you're lying."

Chapter Fourteen

I had a really hard time saying good-bye to Sam at the airport on Sunday. I probably wasn't going to see her more than once before Christmas break. She promised to come back for Jack's big Halloween party, but she had too much going on with work and school to take the time to travel. She was having to deal with the Laine Hotel in San Francisco on the weekends while her parents were in Europe. I was jealous that she got to spend the weekends in S.F. I'd never been there but was sure there were plenty of beautiful lesbians willing to make Sam feel welcome. It just wasn't feasible for me to fly out there; catching a late flight on a Friday and coming home on a Sunday would leave me no time to grade papers, much less pack up the house and get ready for the big move.

I admit to being a little resentful about having to deal with the move myself. Of course, it was my house and all my belongings that I had to deal with; Sam had her stuff in storage. Most of the paperwork would be taken care of; all we had to do was sign, write a check and the house was ours. I was really struggling with the fact that I would be living in our new house alone. Sam was on her last semester, but she did have distractions that could take her anywhere. She was already scheduled to be in London in January for some family thing. She was supposed to be in San Francisco for Thanksgiving and hadn't really made any promises that she would for sure be home for Christmas.

She had an offer from a local Dallas firm, but she hadn't committed yet. I was terrified that some big law firm in New York or Boston would try to recruit her. She assured me that as long as she owned the Dallas Laine that her place was in Dallas. I prayed that her parents didn't give her a hotel in Singapore as a graduation gift just to get her away from me. They were very accepting of our relationship, but I often got the feeling that they wanted someone a little more "polished" for their precious princess. I mentioned that to Sam once, and she told me that I was mistaken. They actually wanted someone a little more "Polish."

There were so many ifs ahead of us that I couldn't wait for the day when Sam was home for good. It seemed like it would be forever, which was why the airport scene about killed me. We stood near the ticket counter as long as we could just staring in silence. I felt a lump in my throat that I had never felt during previous good-byes. I knew I wasn't going to cry, but I was afraid to speak. Finally, they called her flight and it was time to go.

I said, "Okay, you'd better run. You still have to get through security."

"Yeah." She wouldn't look up at me.

"I'm gonna miss you, Sammy." I reached for her hand.

"Me too. We have a lifetime ahead of us. It's just a few more months." She took my hand.

"I know, but my world works so much better when you're close."

"Mine too." She reached into her briefcase. "I got you something."

I took the box from her hand and opened it. Inside was a pair of red cashmere socks. "These are beautiful. A little weird, but very nice, thank you."

"I bought myself the same pair. We have matching socks."

"Okay . . ." I didn't get the symbolism.

"Maybe one day we can get married and it will all make sense to you." She smiled as if holding back some incredible joke.

"Alrighty then. You go now, and call me tonight. Have a safe trip."

"And you have a safe drive." She set down her briefcase and held open her arms.

We shared a long passionate kiss right there in the American Airlines terminal. The kiss meant so much more to me when I felt the tears on her face. I tried to cry, to show that I was sad too, but nothing came.

She gathered her things and headed to the gate. She never turned around, but I heard her shout. "I love you with all my heart, doctor!"

"I love you too, counselor!" I shouted back, and she was gone.

I thought about the sock thing for the first twenty minutes of the ride home. Nothing came to me, but I knew there had to be something significant about the gift. I turned on the radio and sang along for a while. As I got back to town and rounded the corner to my house, it finally struck me. Two pairs of matching socks and her remark, "Maybe one day we can get married and it will all make sense to you." It was as plain as day; she was planning a "Same Socks Marriage." I laughed myself to sleep that night and wore the socks the next day.

❧

Mid-October was upon us and moving day finally arrived. The movers were to arrive at ten, and I figured I'd have Sarah's new house emptied and cleaned out by six. Of course, with the unpredictable Texas weather, a massive storm hit. We were under tornado watches and flash flood warnings. According to the Weather Channel, everything was supposed to clear up by noon, which meant absolutely nothing since the day before they had predicted clear skies and high temperatures. Loading the truck wasn't the problem; they just backed up to the garage and took everything out the back way. The problem was that the storm was so bad that there was no visibility on the highway. The moving company refused to send their guys on the road until the rain slowed. I called them a bunch of wusses and threatened to drive the truck myself. They were not amused. Everything was loaded by one, and I managed to get the house totally spotless and looking new by the time the rain stopped at four.

I loaded up my luggage and necessities, which included my cat, and took a final look around. A million memories popped into my head, and for a moment I thought that maybe moving was a bad idea. I remembered the day I found the house, and how Jack helped me move in and get settled. I could still see him on the ladder two weeks later trying to run from a little mouse that came in from the garage. I thought about Amy's visits and how we would sit up all night talking and watching old movies. I remembered the Saturday afternoon parties I hosted for the university staff; we'd get a little tipsy and watch college football, jealous that our woman's college didn't have a team. I could still feel the warmth I felt the day I came home after getting promoted to department head. I was so proud of my little house, and I was so in love with the neighborhood.

There were two memories that resonated in my mind. They

were probably two of the best moments of my life. The first was the night I met Sam; she and Toby walked me home and we made a date right there on the front porch. The other was the first night that Sam and I made love in the house. I tried so hard to get her to sleep at my place instead of the hotel. She spent half the night going through my CDs and books, and the other half making me the happiest woman on earth. It was those memories, the thoughts of Sam, that made me walk out the door. I realized right then and there that as much as I loved that house and everything it meant to me, my life with Sam, our future, was all I wanted in life. Our future was in Dallas, in an amazing bungalow, and I couldn't wait to get there. I closed the door behind me, placed the key under the mat and prayed that Jules and Sarah would find as much happiness as I did in that house.

I followed the moving truck all the way to Dallas. I don't know why they were so concerned about driving in the rain. The driver never went above 45 when the road was dry. Fortunately, they unloaded the truck a lot faster than they loaded, and they were paid and on their way by eight. I sat in that huge quiet house feeling a bit lonely. I heard some weird noises and spooked myself. I realized that a house that old could possibly contain ghosts. My imagination took over and I became increasingly curious about whether or not Camille's grandmother actually died in the house. I grabbed my cell in search of affirmation.

"Sam? Do you believe in ghosts?"

"Yes, I do. I believe in Santa Claus too, and I know that you believe in the Easter Bunny. So it goes to show that what we believe in can be pretty harmless. I take it you're at the new house?"

"Yeah, there was a bit of a rain delay, but everything went pretty smoothly. They broke my desk chair and scratched up the sides of the big TV."

"No biggie. We can sue them. Are Jules and Sarah moving in today?"

"No, not until tomorrow. They had barely even started packing when I talked to them this morning. Jules has her apartment until the end of the month. Is it weird that I'm gonna miss my old house?"

"Of course not. You had a great life there, but you'll still see the house when we visit the lovebirds."

"It won't be the same. Kitty won't be there."

"Oh, here we go again. Home is where the cat is." She laughed. "Where is the little four-legged object of your obsession right now?"

"He's sniffing around. I think there must be a strong scent of Rob's poodle imbedded in the hardwoods. Kitty took a bath in the bedroom fireplace when we first got here. I hear a lot of creepy noises. I think I need to hook up the stereo to drown them out."

"Is Jack coming over tonight?"

"I'm supposed to call him. Maybe I can get him to spend the night. He felt really bad about not helping with the move today."

"Well, it was rather convenient, his having the office open today."

"He does it one Saturday a month for that government program. It was coincidental that it happened to be this particular Saturday."

"Uh-huh. I'm kidding. I feel bad that I wasn't there to help either."

"I'll pay you back. When you get your shit out of storage, I'll pretend to have a hernia."

"Deal. You know, it could be kind of fun to have a ghost or two in the house. We could have a séance and conjure up some dead—" She stopped midsentence. "I'm sorry, Doc. I'm sure you don't want to conjure up any spirits."

"It's okay. If I thought I could actually find a way to talk to Amy, I'd try it. She would have loved this house, and she totally believed in ghosts. We used to sneak down to the basement, hold flashlights under our chins and tell stupid ghost stories."

"Oh, the fun we all had as kids, scaring the hell out of each other," Sam added.

"Kids? This was just last year when we went up for Mom and Dad's anniversary. Poor Jack got so scared that he shot beer out of his nose. I thought the poor guy was gonna pee his pants."

"Ooh, he's a chicken boy. You could have some fun with him tonight if he sleeps over. Exaggerate the noises and tell him you swore you saw something."

"Oh, that's awful. I think I'll do it." I loved the idea.

"Doc, you aren't scared, are you?"

"No, not really. I feel pretty safe here. It's a wonderful house. I think we done good, kiddo."

"Why do you think Amy would have liked it?"

"The tile. She was always impressed by those little one-inch tiles you see a lot of in New Mexico. She would have loved the pattern of the tiles in the bathrooms and kitchen. Plus, I could totally see her sliding across the floors in her slippers." It occurred to me that I was talking about Amy and not getting sad.

It had apparently occurred to Sam as well. "I think this is the first time you've talked about Amy to me in a long, long time. I like hearing about her."

"Yeah. It's funny, I'm actually happy today. Amy would have been happy for me. Instead of thinking about the fact that she's gone, I'm picturing her as if she were here. Does that make sense?"

"It kinda does. It's getting late. Why don't you go call the scaredy cat and plan your scare tactics. I'll call you in the morning. There's a luncheon at the hotel, so I'll call you before then."

"I forgot to ask, how is San Francisco treating you?"

"It's not bad. I had to miss a class and fly in early—there was some electrical problem. I was hoping to make it out last night, but I didn't get a break."

"Ah, I'm sorry," I lied. "The lesbian community must be really disappointed."

"You aren't worried about that, are you?"

"Nah, you've got a home in Dallas. A beautiful home, I might add. I have a feeling your heart and body are anxious to come back to Dallas."

"Your feeling is right. I can't wait. Go toy with Jack and sleep well."

I unpacked my luggage and a few boxes while I waited for my brother to arrive. When I called him, he promised to spend the night and bring the beer and pizza. I had a plan of my own. I put an old glass on the edge of the counter and rubbed some catnip on it. I knew that once Kitty got a whiff, he would rub his face all over the glass, knocking it off the counter to the floor. I locked the cat in the bedroom and plotted to let him out about an hour after Jack arrived. That would give me enough time to bring up the noises and make Jack a little nervous. I put a few other things on the counter so he wouldn't give the lone glass a second thought. I turned the CD player on softly to be sure he could hear the crash of the glass over the music.

He arrived around ten. "Hey, lady, how's the new pad?"

"Jack, no one's called it a 'pad' since nineteen seventy-seven. Now a pad has wings and refers to—"

"Okay! I got it. How is the new house?"

"I love it. So much history, so solid. I even think there may be a ghost or two here."

"Oh, ha ha. The joke's on ol' Jack. You know how I hate ghost stories."

"I know. All I'm saying is that I've heard a few noises. No biggie. Let's have some pizza and a few beers." I grabbed the box and led him into the living room.

"Seriously, sis, don't fuck with me. I've had an awful day. I don't need to top it off with pissing my pants from a ghost story." He frowned.

Suddenly I felt really bad about my plan but decided to continue until I felt real concern for his day. "What happened? Why was it awful?"

"Well, my first patient had a heart attack, but she survived—probably in part to my CPR skills. Then I had lunch with Camille, and things went sour by dessert. We are officially broken up."

"I'm sorry, Jack. Did you tell her you weren't compatible?"

"No. Actually, she told me I was lazy."

"Wow, you went to dentistry school and opened your own practice. What does she want?"

"She wants a football player."

"Seriously?"

"Yes, she met a Cowboys' lineman, and since they practice every day and work out all the time, they are anything but lazy."

"I'm sorry. Guess you should have told her about your football scholarship."

"Nah, she's shallow. Whatever. A toast to your new home." He held out his bottle of beer.

"May there be passion, and may the ghosts be friendly."

"Doc, I'm serious. Don't fuck with me."

He seemed adamant, which made me decide to drop my little scheme. "Okay. I'll give it a rest. I have heard a few squeaks, but I'm sure it's just from the old foundation. I admit that I did have a plan, but I concede. I will not fuck with you."

"Okay, thanks. There's been enough CPR for one day in my life."

"Sorry about your patient and about Camille. Got any other

female prospects on the horizon?"

"As far as females go, I currently have three loves. My memories, Sam and you. Although there is a drink cart girl at the country club."

"Oh, I've seen her. I hate to say this, but she plays for our team." The girl flashed into my mind, and I remembered her short spiky hair and how she wore shorts with hiking boots.

"No! Don't say that!"

"Yeah, she gave me her phone number when I was at the range last month. Sorry."

"Not the first time you've stolen a woman away from me." He laughed.

"True. But you've had your share of theft."

"What? I've never."

I took a sip of my beer. "Oh, come on. Do you remember Veronica Ellis?"

"Yes, she was my prom date."

"Yeah, well, I had a major crush on her."

"You might have had more luck. I took her to the Best Western on prom night and she told me that I wasn't her type." He opened another beer.

"I don't think I was her type either, though. I tried to kiss her at your graduation party and she told me that *I* wasn't her type." I laughed.

"How funny. I wonder what her type was?"

"Honestly? I heard a rumor that she was arrested for bestiality."

"Dude, that's wrong." He kicked me.

"Jack, the sad thing is that I'm serious. She's no longer allowed to go near sheep farms in her town."

"Oh, my . . . you know, I think I did . . ."

Just then a loud crash came from the kitchen. Jack and I sat there frozen, each of us waiting for the other to investigate.

"Shit. Jack, I swear that wasn't part of my plan."

"Doc, fuck, what the hell was that?"

"It was a breaking glass, but I have no idea how it fell off the counter." I was actually terrified. I wanted my old house back, and I wanted to know what the hell had happened to Camille's grandmother.

"Go see what it was." He urged me toward the kitchen.

"No, you go see. You're the man."

"It's your house, jackass."

I slowly made my way to the kitchen, holding a beer bottle up-side down in my hand for protection. When I entered the empty kitchen, I saw my befuddled cat sitting on the counter and a broken glass on the floor. I was totally relieved but completely confused. I went back to the living room and found Jack laughing his ass off.

"What's so funny? You're the chicken." I was a bit mad.

"I'm sorry. Was the cat scared? I hope he wasn't injured."

I realized that he must have known my plan. "Okay, what gave it away?"

"Well, Doc, every time I visit you, that damn cat won't leave me alone. Tonight, when I arrive, he's nowhere to be found. When you went to put the beer in the fridge, I let him out of your room."

"Okay. But how did you know that it was the cat who made the noise. It could have been a ghost."

"Yeah, but Sam called and warned me that you would try to scare me. I was prepared for anything. She was hoping to scare the shit out of you instead. Did it work?"

"Hardy har har. You guys win. I almost peed. You are an ass, and Sam is officially on my shit list. Revenge is sweet, so you both better look out."

"You got a sharp lady there. I hope you keep each other on your toes." Jack grinned.

"On our toes, among other things." I grinned back.

Chapter Fifteen

Jack and I decided that it would be more fun to have the big Halloween party in our sparsely furnished bungalow than his modern townhouse. We thought the creaky floors and rumors of ghosts would add to the Halloween theme. Plus, with hardly any furnishings in place at the new house, there was plenty of room for a plethora of costumed drunks.

Jack planned on dressing in his usual Sweet Transvestite costume. He had been dieting and working out for a month in preparation. I questioned his sexuality multiple times, reminding him that most straight men don't care how they look in garters. I had no idea what costume to wear. Sam and I thought about going as the *Rocky Horror* maids, but I didn't want to mess with all that makeup. Sam settled on dressing as a Victoria's Secret angel . . . which thrilled me to no end. She encouraged me to do the same, but I couldn't see myself sporting lingerie in front of my friends and new neighbors. I had lost weight in my depression, but not enough to compete with Sam's muscular frame.

Finally, with a day to spare, I settled on the easiest costume I could think of—Catholic schoolgirl. I got online and found the sweater, skirt, shoes, socks and shirt and had them sent overnight. I didn't tell Sam about my costume for fear she would be disappointed with my conservative choice, or else shocked by my blasphemy. I actually thought a nun would be a better choice, as we used to make a lot of nun jokes, but I couldn't find a suitable habit online.

We spent two days preparing the house with every haunted house accessory available in Dallas. We strung cobwebs over anything that didn't move, had mummy and Frankenstein statues strategically placed throughout the inside and even put pumpkin lights all over the front of the house. Outside, it looked like a very distorted Christmas scene. Inside, it looked like an old Vincent Price movie set. I was actually a little creeped out by whole thing. Caterers from the hotel brought by a hearty buffet and full bar, which included bartenders. They thought of everything, including eyeball appetizers and steaming green punch. Everything was in place for our housewarming/Halloween extravaganza.

Trick-or-treaters started knocking around six. I was astonished by the number of kids in our neighborhood. We went through two bowls of candy before seven. Our adult guests were to arrive at eight, so at seven thirty, we retreated to our room to dress and let the bartenders handle the candy and door. Sam locked herself in the closet while I put on my costume in the bathroom. I was happy with the results. Personally, I thought I looked a little sexy with my little round glasses and insignia sweater. The definition of the word *sexy* completely changed when Sam exited the closet. She wore a white lace eyelet corset, white garters, white heels and huge white angel wings. Her hair, looking windblown, fell around her face . . . well . . . like an angel.

I about fell to my knees. "Well, hello, Angel."

"Hello, Mary Katherine." She beamed.

"My word. Maybe we should cancel the party and go straight to bed," I said while petting her soft, feathery wings.

"I'm sorry. I can't go to bed with a schoolgirl." She peeked under my skirt. "Nice boxer shorts, although a little disappointing."

"I could take them off," I whispered in her ear and smelled her delicate perfume.

"Yes, why don't you do that." She lifted my skirt as I pulled my plaid boxers down over my loafers.

"Shall we retreat to the bed?" I kissed her shoulder.

"I'm afraid I'll damage my wings." She led me to the bathroom counter and hiked up my skirt. "Have a seat."

I pulled myself up on the counter and spread my legs. Just as Sam was getting on her knees, Jack barged through the unlocked bathroom door.

"Oh, my gawd!" He covered his eyes. "If this was anyone but my sister I'd be in . . . well . . . heaven, angels and all." He laughed and shut the door. "Holy shit!" he yelled from the other side, still laughing. "Your guests are starting to arrive. Shall I send them home?"

"No, we'll be out in a minute," I shouted back.

"Um, make that five minutes," Sam called and went back to her knees.

By ten, the party was in full swing. Our new house was filled with drag queens, ghosts, biker babes and superheroes; I even think the Village People made an appearance. Tired of fighting off the gay boys, Jack decided to change out of the lingerie and into some scrubs. He had already won the contest for best costume and was thrilled with his prize bottle of Scotch.

"Hey, bro. Sorry about earlier." I leaned into him while we danced.

"My fault. I should know by now to knock around you guys. Sometimes I forget that you're a couple."

"Well, I hope the image of my . . . um . . . position isn't burned into your brain forever."

"Don't worry. I'm a doctor. I see things like that all the time."

"Jack, you're a dentist. You'd better not see anything like that at work."

"Oh, yeah. Still, I can handle it. If it had been Sam half naked on the counter . . . well, I might consider stealing her away."

"My team, my girl." I motioned toward Catwoman in the corner. "That lady over there has been watching you all night. Maybe you should dance with her."

"I noticed that one earlier. She's beautiful, for a man, isn't she?"

"Damn! It's getting so I can't even recognize my friends. Is that David?"

"No . . . it's Tobias!"

"You're kidding me. We didn't know he was coming. Has Sam seen him yet?"

"No, he told me to keep quiet. He was dying to see if his sister noticed him dressed as a kitty superhero."

"I've got an idea. I think it's time to mess with Sammy to-night." I kissed his cheek and walked off.

When I found Sam, she was deep in conversation with Jules and Sarah about the importance of washing your hands immediately after grocery shopping—before putting the groceries away. I waited patiently for a break in conversation then stole Sam away, grabbing another beer as we passed the bar.

"Oh, thank God you saved me. I thought I was gonna die

when they told me how they put Purell on the shopping cart. Not just the handle, mind you. The top part where their purses sit. Argh!" She took a big sip of her whiskey sour.

"What are they dressed as, anyway? Laurel and Hardy?" I stared their way.

"What? You don't recognize Bob and Bill from *Tipping the Velvet*?" She laughed.

"Ah. A recognizable costume for anyone who can afford premium cable."

"Don't forget, Sarah works at a cable company. You know, she is becoming a little pretentious, and I think Jules is starting to get annoyed. You should talk to her later."

"Talk to whom? Sarah or Jules?"

"Yes. Both, either. I don't care. Just keep them away from me. What did you wrangle me outside for . . . you got a light?" She popped a cigarette into her mouth.

"First of all, you don't smoke." I took the Marlboro and lit it for myself. "Have you ever considered a threesome?"

"You know I have." Sam blushed and put her hand on my hip.

"Well, if I found someone I thought we'd both like, would you make the proposition?"

"I guess a few more drinks and I could be convinced. Who's the poor soul you've chosen to be our sex slave . . . please don't say Sarah. She's freaking me out."

"No, not Sarah. Ick." I glanced inside at Catwoman. "I was thinking about the kitty in the corner over there." I tried hard not to laugh.

Sam took a long look and fought a smile. I thought she was intrigued. "Well, Doc, I'm not sure which is more shocking to me. The fact that you want to have sex with a man, or the fact that you want to have sex with my brother." She continued to fight the smile.

"Damn it! You knew he was here? I thought I could set up a nice embarrassment for both of you." I flicked my cigarette into the firepit.

"First I saw him at the bar; no one else asks for three cherries in a screwdriver. Then I noticed him about an hour ago when he and Jack were talking. Then I noticed all the men and women who were hitting on him. I figured he really wanted out of the costume, so I decided to make him sweat it out until midnight. Nice try, though."

"They're playing our song." I heard "The Monster Mash" coming from inside the house. "Wanna dance?"

She took my hand and we went inside to the living room just in time to see Jules throw her bourbon in Sarah's face. I really wanted to ignore the situation and go back outside, but the party more or less stopped and I realized I had to intervene.

"Ladies—or should I say, Bill, Bob—what's the problem here?" I stood between them while Sam cleaned the liquor off the hardwoods and handed Sarah a towel for her face.

"She called me a slob," Jules said, louder than necessary.

"You know, throwing your drink doesn't really prove that you're not." I laughed, hoping to ease the tension.

"She called me a snob." Sarah sounded like an adolescent tattling on her sibling.

"Okay, Sam, how about you and I take the slob and the snob outside for a smoke break?"

Sam gracefully stood and brushed off her wings. "Okay, ladies and gentleman, nothing to see here. Please go back to your Halloween fun. Oh, and whoever left the used condom on the bathroom floor has five minutes to clean it up or I'm sending it out for DNA testing." As three men in leather headed for the bathroom and everyone laughed hysterically, she added, "The joke's on them. I was kidding about finding a condom."

Everyone stayed and danced until three a.m.

❧

Oh, the fantasy every woman has at least once in her life. Every gay woman anyway. A girl in a school uniform and a girl in white lingerie and heels seduce each other by the soft firelight in the bedroom of their new house. The possibilities are endless: heels on, plaid skirt hiked up, angel wings tossed across the bedpost, tequila shots off the schoolgirl's belly, the soft insignia sweater pulled slowly over her head. Oh, my . . . that would have been nice.

Instead, as we kissed our way to the bedroom after all the guests had either left or settled in sleeping bags in the den, we found Sarah passed out on our bed and Jules on the floor by the dying fire. The sound of their synchronized snoring drowned out the sound of our disappointed groans.

"No freaking way. I thought they were going to the hotel with Toby," I said with sadness in my tone and my lips curled in a puppy dog pout.

"I thought they were too, but I think Toby went home with Monica." She looked outside. His Jeep was parked in the driveway. "We should have called them a cab. It's our own fault." She kicked off her heels. "We could move them, you know."

"Nah, let's just throw some pillows on the floor and get some sleep. I have a feeling that we are gonna have some childish drama to deal with in the morning." I sighed and changed into a shirt and boxers.

We lay awake whispering to each other about the evening's events and listened to the soft snores of Bill and Bob.

I awoke around eight, my head pounding and my back killing me from the hard floor. I heard noises in the kitchen and looked around to find that I was alone in the room. I took the time to take a shower, brush my teeth and get dressed, hoping that our guests might clear out by the time I was done. I heard the front door close as I exited the bedroom and breathed a sigh of relief. I realized my sigh was in vain when I found Sam sitting on the kitchen counter with Sarah and Jules.

"I thought you guys would be on your way home by now. I thought I heard someone leave."

"Lara and Ricky just took off. They were so hung over—I thought they both might puke." Sam batted her eyelashes and shot me a crooked smile. "Jules and Sarah have decided to stay for breakfast." I sensed a lack of patience in her voice. Jules and Sarah were obviously too young to appreciate the importance of leaving when the fun was over.

"Well, sorry we don't have any furniture. We do have eggs and bagels though. Anyone want coffee?" I reached for the warm carafe and offered it around. Sam took the initiative to start cooking breakfast while I climbed onto the countertop. I had a flashback to the previous night's bathroom counter scene and got lightheaded. "So, did you two sleep well?"

"Passed out is more like it. I was pretty tipsy," Jules said while holding her head.

"I slept fine. I wore more alcohol than I drank," Sarah added sarcastically.

"I slept like the angel that I am." Sam made a halo motion above her head.

"Sorry about throwing my drink, Sarah." Jules spoke in monotone. Even I didn't believe the apology was heartfelt.

"Whatever, Jules," she said in the same monotone, not making eye contact.

"Alrighty. How do you want your eggs, ladies?" Sam changed the subject.

"I like mine poached," Sarah answered.

"Of course you do. You can't just say scrambled and make it

easy for her," Jules whispered.

"I'll just have coffee. Thank you, Sam."

"Okay, poached for Sarah, sunnyside up for my sunshine lady and fried for me."

"Do you guys want us to leave so you can talk?" I really hoped they would say yes.

"Actually, I'd like Sarah to leave." Jules spoke sternly.

"Really? You want me to go, do you?" She hopped off the counter.

"Okay, no one is leaving just yet. Let's talk this out like adults." I lit a cigarette.

Jules snapped. "There's only three adults in this room. The other one is a spoiled brat."

"Okay, Jules. That's not gonna help the situation." Sam threw a bagel at her. "Don't say something you'll regret later."

I flashed back to my early twenties and wondered if I would have been mature enough to handle a relationship like theirs. They'd fast taken on a mortgage and all the pressures of couple-dom. To make matters worse, they had never been with other women. They jumped into the relationship on the possibility that it was the girl thrill and not true love. It occurred to me that maybe Sam and I had pushed them too hard. After all, we didn't know anything about either one of them, and we were practically forcing them to be together. I decided that I should stick my big nose in and try to be the voice of reason.

"Okay, Sarah. What's your beef with Jules? What do you want to say to her? Please be civil. I'm too hung over to deal with a catfight." I threw my cigarette in the sink.

"I don't have a beef with her. I don't have anything with her. I don't want to be like this anymore."

"Be like what?" Jules persisted.

"Gay, different, alternative, a dyke, a carpet-muncher." She seemed livid.

"Okay, no name-calling. Some of my best friends munch carpets on a daily basis." Sam was obviously trying to sound glib.

"Sorry, Sam. I'm just tired of living a double life, of playing the pronoun game, of lying to my friends and family and co-workers about my 'roommate situation.'"

I leaned forward and said sternly, "I know it's tough. But if you don't want to live a lie, maybe it's best to face the truth of who you are and be open to everyone about your relationship."

"I don't want to be gay. I want to be normal like everyone else." She started crying.

I was a little offended by her remark, as it implied that we weren't normal. Although I did know where she was coming from. I had struggled with the same emotions and used to beg God to make me like all straight women in the world. Hell, I fought it so hard that I married a man, and I still hadn't told my parents about my homosexuality.

"Sarah, nobody *wants* to be different. No one wants to spend her life feeling like she isn't normal. But you will eventually find that once you've accepted who you are, and live that lifestyle every day, you will find the normalcy you are looking for. Being gay doesn't define you. It's a small part of who you are," I explained.

Sam stepped in, "For me, Sarah, I was fortunate to be out to my family very early on. I never had to struggle with things like you and Doc, or try to hide myself from friends. But the thing is, I would think that one day you'll be so used to the way things are, to coming home to Jules, that you can't imagine your life any other way. I know I like how my life is. I like the lifestyle."

"Sam's right." I smiled. "I love being gay, and at this point in my life, I wouldn't want it any other way. If they came out with a pill that would make me straight . . . I wouldn't take it. It doesn't define me, but it is part of me, and I love that part of me."

Jules, who had sat silent so far, finally spoke up. "Sarah, maybe you're not gay, or maybe I'm not the one for you. If you don't feel it strong enough to make me the priority over what your coworkers might say, then maybe this isn't the relationship for you." She seemed surprisingly calm.

Sarah stared at the floor as we all waited for her to speak. "I don't know. I just don't know. How can anyone be *sure* they're gay?"

Sam and I said at the same time, "You just know."

"Is it possible that I'm bisexual?" Sarah blushed.

"Do you think about men? So you look at men!" Jules appeared angry.

"No, not really. But to be honest, baby, I do think about other women. I look at other women, and sometimes I even fantasize about other women. Is that normal?"

The three of us remained quiet, waiting for the others to answer. Finally, after what seemed like an eternity, Sam came to the rescue. "It's normal to have a passing fantasy. I admit that I'm guilty of turning my head to watch a beautiful woman walk by. The thing is, I know in my heart that Doc is the one who gets me hot, who makes me feel at home. She's my biggest fantasy."

"So maybe I'm not the one for you. Maybe I was just your first." Jules was still relatively calm.

"Well, Jules, am I really the one for you? Can you picture us together when we're as old as Doc and Sam?"

"Um, careful there. We really aren't that old. In fact, Sam's actually closer to your age than you might think." I lit another cigarette.

Sarah looked Sam over and said, "Really? You're my age? Maybe we should go out sometime."

"That's not funny, Sarah. I don't know if I am the one for you. Honestly, I can't picture us together in ten years. Lately I'm amazed that we made it this far."

Sarah reached for the coffeepot. "Jules, I'm amazed too. I think maybe we got caught up in being each other's first. You

know, the thrill of finally being with a woman. I'm almost positive that I'm gay. And I'm almost positive that you and I aren't
meant to be." She spoke as if it were a rehearsed speech.

"I have to agree. I've slept with you. I know you're gay. But I
also know that we can't keep forcing this to work. I think it's best
if we just be friends."

The room fell silent again.

"Girls, the fact that neither one of you is crying means that
this is the right decision. You're both being mature and admitting
the truth about your feelings. I bet you really will remain friends,
probably for life. Now get out of my house so I can seduce my
girlfriend before she heads to the airport." I winked at Sam. "I'm
kidding. You can finish your breakfast first."

So that was the end of that. Jules and Sarah were a couple no
more. But by the time they finished their breakfast, they were
both laughing like the best of friends. I think I was the only one
sad to see it end.

Chapter Sixteen

Thanksgiving break was approaching, Sam was out in California, and I had no plans for the holiday. I had many invitations but declined them all. Sam wouldn't make it back to Dallas due to hotel business in San Francisco. I had absolutely no desire to head West to be with her. Well, I wanted to be with her, but more so, I wanted to be alone. The date of Amy's memorial service was a few weeks away, and the thought of that only reminded me that she wouldn't be around for Thanksgiving.

I submerged myself in work and used it as an excuse for everything. Jules and Sarah, who had remained roommates—in separate rooms—invited me to dinner. I told them I had papers to grade. Jack invited me to a Cowboys' game; I told him I had lectures to write. Some of the other teachers invited me to a department happy hour, and as much as I tried, I couldn't use work as an excuse to bail out. They knew me and my schedule too well and wouldn't take no for an answer.

I dreaded the outing all week and had to force myself to be cheerful with my secretary on the ride over to the local Bennigan's. We arrived around four and it was pretty empty, even for a Friday. I was relieved and hoped maybe the others had decided not to show. Unfortunately, half an hour later, the entire English Department faculty filled the bar area. As head of the department, I felt the obligation to mingle, but as a depressed woman, I also felt the need to stay seated and drown my sorrows in my beer.

My secretary, Jana, aware of my situation, tried her best to make me laugh. Bless her heart, she was like a one-woman stand-up routine. She told me jokes, did impressions, ragged on the people around us and even tried singing. I didn't budge. I smiled politely and sipped my drink.

Just when I thought Jana had finally given up, she threw a Hail Mary. "Hey, Doc. I was hoping you'd have some fun to-night. Maybe I should tell Richard that you want to go home with him. Will that make you smile?"

"Will sex with Richard make me smile?" I didn't know whether to laugh or cry. Richard was three times my age and a bit sweaty. "Um, no. But thanks for playing."

"Okay, Doc. How about if I tell Millie that you want to go home with her?" She smiled like a cat eating chicken.

I couldn't help but smile. I looked over at Millie, a beautiful older Jamaican woman, and I blushed. "She has a better chance than Richard." I hoped that sounded noncommittal.

"I knew it!" Jana tossed a swizzle stick at me and did a little chair dance.

"You knew what?" I honestly didn't care if she found out about my lifestyle.

"I knew you thought Richard was disgusting." She winked

and pursed her lips. "Don't worry. I won't tell a soul."

Despite that little conversation, my Bennigan's adventure seemed a bit boring to me. But the evening actually did turn out well, and I even had a change in my perspective that night. It wasn't a colleague who got to me that night, but a total stranger. After we finished a round of appetizers and several drinks, people started clearing out. Jana was my ride and she wanted to hang around to see if her waiter boyfriend would get off work soon. We ordered another round and she sneaked back to the kitchen to find him. I sat alone at the little pub table and gulped my frosty pint. I had decided that if I was going to be out, I might as well be drunk.

A few minutes later, a drunk kid came and sat at my little table. My first reaction was to be annoyed and send him away. Then I noticed his T-shirt, which read, "Billings High School Football." My heart jumped at the odd reminder of Amy.

"Hey, my sister says you're her English teacher." He didn't sound as drunk as he appeared.

"Oh, yeah, who's your sister?"

He motioned to a booth by the door and she waved. "I wanted to thank you. She used to drive my parents nuts with her terrible grammar. She used to say things like 'me and Joe' or 'him and me.' Now she thinks a little before she speaks."

"Well, I'm just doing my job, but I'm glad she got something from the class." I forced a smile.

He stood to leave and I grabbed his arm. Something in my heart told me I had to ask about the Billings shirt. I think I startled him because he stared at me for the longest time. "Don't I know you?" he asked.

"Well, I work at the university." I was still holding his arm. I couldn't seem to let go.

He raised his eyebrows. "No, I know you from home. You live in that white house over on Forest Avenue."

I knew immediately what he meant and my heart raced. "You're from Billings?"

"Yes. I'm just visiting my sister for Thanksgiving. You're Miss O'Connor. I mow your lawn. Don't you remember me?" He grinned and held out his hand.

I didn't know how to react. I shook his hand and held on to it. He was a connection to my sister. He was a third party who knew Amy. The coincidence was surreal—no, impossible—but I held on to the warmth of the touch and fought back tears. "That's my twin sister, Amy."

"No way! What are the odds of that!" He was practically shouting. "I'm Joe."

"Nice to meet you, Joe. I'm Dani." The sound of my own name resonated in my head and seemed like an old friend.

"Well, how's your sister? I haven't seen her in a while. Someone said she moved."

"Amy's . . ." I fought the lump in my throat. "Amy passed away seven months ago." It felt so odd, yet so real, to finally give a time frame with the statement.

"Oh, my." His voice squeaked. "I am so sorry to hear that. I had no idea. Oh, boy, am I sorry."

"Thank you, Joe. I'm sorry too." I stared at him and found his gaze to be very soothing.

"Was it sudden?"

"She had been sick for a while. Cancer got her."

"It must be hard to lose a sister." He glanced affectionately toward the booth by the door.

"Just love her, and be good to her." I motioned toward his sister.

"I'll do that. Again, I am really sorry to hear about Amy. That's a real shame. She was a really nice lady. She tipped me well and even gave me a beer once."

"That sounds like my Amy. Okay, you get back to your sister,

Joe. It was wonderful and amazing running into you." I kissed his cheek.

"It's a small world. I took care of your sister's lawn and you took care of my sister's language. Sounds like a good trade. Perhaps we're soul mates?"

"That's a great trade. And our souls are definitely linked somehow. Thank you, Joe."

He stood and started to walk away. Suddenly he turned and kissed me full on the lips. Then he shot me a crooked smile and went back to his seat.

It occurred to me that I finally kissed a younger man. Then it struck me that I had just kissed someone connected to Amy. I felt warm inside and felt a smile grow on my face.

Later that night on the phone, Sam could tell a difference in my demeanor.

"Did you have fun at happy hour?"

"Not really. My coworkers are a bunch of literate nerds."

"Well, take me to their leader." She laughed.

That struck me as terribly funny and I actually chuckled for a good minute.

"Tell me, professor. Why do you actually sound so happy if you had such an awful night?"

"Well, counselor, I too have kissed a younger man."

"Really?" She didn't sound upset, just merely intrigued. "How did it feel?"

"It was the warm fuzzy I've been craving." I went on to tell her the entire unbelievable story and she was equally awed. That's why I loved Sam so much. She shared my milestones, and my triumphs meant as much to her as they did to me.

Chapter Seventeen

I decided not to boycott Thanksgiving. I knew Jack was feeling a bit sad too, so I took him up on his offer to spend the day together. Neither one of us wanted to cook, so we made reservations at the Laine Hotel restaurant. After my last class on Tuesday, my cell phone rang. It was Jack with a proposition. He figured that if we were going to have turkey at the Laine anyway, it might as well be the Laine in San Francisco. I agreed that it made more sense to be with Sam in California than with her parents at the Dallas hotel.

"We'll never get a flight out," I said. "Everyone booked months in advance, and I can't afford a last-minute ticket anyway."

"I knew you'd say that. I've already made arrangements. Get back to Dallas and pack and I'll pick you up at seven." Jack had that protective sound in his voice.

"What about Kitty? I can't leave him alone."

Jack had the answer for that too. "Toby's in town. He said he would stay at your house, since the alternative was being under his parents' watchful eyes for five days."

The minute I hung up the phone, I raced back to Dallas, cleaned up the house for Toby and packed a suitcase. Ten minutes till seven, Jack arrived at my door.

I looked outside and saw Sam's Porsche parked out front. "How on earth did you get the Boxter? She loves that car more than she loves me."

"Not true, lady. She loves you more. When I called her and told her my plan, she suggested that a road trip would be more fun in a convertible sports car."

"Road trip? Are you serious? You want to drive to California and back in five days?"

"No, just to California. We're gonna fly back and Sam will drive the car home after she graduates. You'll fly out to join her, of course. Frankly, she was thrilled to find a way to get the car out there. She was tired of driving her aunt's old Honda. I can't believe she survived this long without a convertible in that weather."

"She should have thought of this when she went out there for school in the first place." I kissed Kitty good-bye, left a key under the mat and loaded my suitcase into Sam's second love. I was ready for an adventure and there was no place more I wanted to be than on my way into Sam's arms. We had about eighteen hundred miles to drive and Jack figured it would take around twenty-six nonstop hours. He'd broken up the driving into roughly two six-hour shifts each. I was to drive to Amarillo, he would get us to Albuquerque, I would take us to Barstow then he would take the last leg on into San Francisco. I was annoyed that I had to drive the first six hours, since I wasn't really prepared for a road trip. He explained that if I drove first, I could sleep the last hours of the journey, thus being well rested for a night with Sam. I didn't argue with his theory. I took us to Starbucks and headed toward 287 toward Amarillo.

Jack was asleep by the time we reached Wichita Falls. I fought sleep by opening the windows; the heavy fog and cold prevented us from putting the top down. I resisted the urge to smoke in Sam's precious car. I knew the nicotine would wake me up, so I pulled over for gas and a cigarette. Jack awoke cranky, complaining that the car was too damned small for his long legs and that we should have brought his SUV. I told him to shut the hell up and go back to sleep. He complied and we were back on the road. We reached Amarillo around one. We were right on schedule, despite the pit stops, for which I credited the speed of the car. A car like that aches to be driven fast.

I pulled over at a Love's Truck Stop and got some coffee for Jack. I stood outside and chain-smoked while Jack used the restroom. I was joined by the truck stop manager who had an adorable smile, and if I had been single and more coherent, I might have flirted with her. Jack came out carrying a bag of road food. Finally wearing a smile, I was ready for my chance to sleep, so I bid farewell to the dimple-faced manager.

We were back on the road, and I was immediately annoyed by the smallness of the convertible. "Damn! These seats really are small."

"Stop complaining and break off a Slim Jim." He held out his hand.

"Let's play a game." I took a bite of the stale meat.

"Okay, Doc. Let's play 'What if.'"

I sat up. "I'll go first. What if we ate salmon on Thanksgiving instead of turkey?"

"Then you'd puke at the smell of seafood every November."

He adjusted the heater. "My turn. What if we had to breathe out of our asses instead of our noses?"

"Then everything would smell like shit." That was easy.

"How would they design cars?"

"How would they design pants?" I laughed.

"Anal sex would be impossible."

"Jack, you're nasty. My turn." I opened a box of Animal Crackers. "What if the sky were red instead of blue?"

"Hmm. That's really deep. I don't think I have an answer for that one. Why do you say 'were red' instead of 'was red'?"

"It's a whole subjunctive tense thing. I'd give you the lecture, but I'm on vacation."

"Maybe I'll audit one of your classes next term. Perhaps I can meet a nice college girl that way." He chuckled. "You get some sleep and I'll wake you in Albuquerque."

"Okay, but if you feel sleepy, pull over. I really don't want to wreck this tiny car."

I adjusted my seat and tried to get comfortable. I couldn't tell if I actually slept or not. I think I was in and out, but who knows if they ever really sleep in a car.

We pulled up in front of the San Francisco Laine Hotel around six o'clock. Adjusting for the time change, the trip only took us about twenty-five hours. Neither of us slept on the last leg of the journey. We were able to put the top down the last four hours of the ride, and I really enjoyed the speed and excitement of the Porsche. Sam was working the check-in desk when we arrived. She had let some employees off for the holiday and left herself a little shorthanded. I thought she looked adorable in her black blazer with nametag. Jack thought she looked like a flight attendant.

I thought I would be more excited to see her, but I was so tired from the trip that I had to force myself to lean over the counter for a kiss. She was busy with the lines of guests, so she just threw the room keys to Jack and told us she got off at eight. I almost felt like we were more of an imposition than a welcomed sight for sore eyes.

Jack and I made ourselves at home in Sam's suite. I took a shower while Jack flipped through every porn channel the hotel had to offer. I told him everyone at the front desk would know he was watching porn, but he didn't seem to care. I wondered if my brother was a big pervert or merely taking advantage of the free movies. After my shower, I found him asleep on the sofa, which proved that he was hardly a porn fanatic or pervert.

Sam got back to the room a little before eight.

"Cut your shift short?" I said, pointing to the clock.

"I had better things to do." She tugged at the belt on my robe and leaned in for a kiss.

"We are not alone." I motioned toward my sleeping brother.

"No, go ahead, it's not like I haven't seen you two go at it before." He sat up and stretched.

I was suddenly rejuvenated by the sight of Sam. It would have been fun, I thought, to have a night on the town, a nice long dinner and maybe a little dancing. "What's on the agenda?"

"I have to work." She pouted for a second and then laughed. "I'm kidding. But we are short-staffed, so I can't get too crazy in case I need to come back here."

"I could stick around here and help out so you two can get crazy," Jack offered. "It's a rare occasion that the two of you are in the same place at once."

"Oh, I couldn't make you do that. You're a guest, and this is your vacation."

"I'm pretty tired. I'd rather stay close to the room tonight anyway. If you have a menial job that needs to be done, I could put in a couple hours."

"We are short two valets." Sam smiled.

"Are you serious? You want me to park cars?" He sounded excited. "I would love that. Can I get a nametag that says 'Brad'?"

"Sure. And you might make some good tips." She turned to me. "But I still need to stay close. How about if we just go to the lobby bar and get some burgers? I promise we can hit the town tomorrow night. Thanksgiving night is pretty slow after the turkey buffet is over."

"Fine with me, but don't expect me to wait tables down there. I refuse to wear those skirts."

"Okay, Brad. Let's go get you a uniform and nametag. No going through the glove boxes, though, and no hot-rodding."

"Damn, you are a real party pooper." He followed her out the door.

Sam and I settled in a corner booth by the front window of the bar. We had a great view of "Brad" and the other valets. The only uniform available was a little tight; he looked a little like Pee-Wee Herman. I had to chuckle every time I saw someone hand him a tip. I was surprised to see him smile as he stuffed the bills into his tight pockets. I guessed that as a dentist, he wasn't used to people tipping him for his work. I wondered how much one would tip a dentist. Ten percent of a crown would be a nice wad of cash. He'd need much bigger pockets in his scrubs.

Sam and I did our best to have an uninterrupted meal. Her two-way radio went off incessantly for the first half-hour, then things started to slow down. We chitchatted about the hotel and her family. She was a bit annoyed to have to cover things while the GM was on sick leave, especially since she had no ownership of the S.F. Laine. I told her that at least things ran so smoothly in

Dallas that they didn't need her. She was still bitter about having to do her father's dirty work.

We lounged for a while sipping margaritas and watching the stream of cars keeping Jack on his toes. A birthday party was ending and he was running all over the place. I hadn't seen him move that fast since college football. Around eleven, a tall blonde pulled up in a black Mercedes. Jack practically knocked over the two other valets while trying to get to her car door. He held out his hand and helped her out, and he didn't let go until she was safely on the curb.

"Who's the blonde, Sam?" I murmured.

"I'm not sure. She checked in last night and was in and out a lot throughout the day." She checked out the car. "Colorado plates. Nice car. Nice legs. But no one I know."

We watched Jack interact with the woman. He was grinning from ear to ear.

"I think he likes her." I smiled.

"Hell, we all like her. Meanwhile she's sitting there thinking, 'Why is this forty-year-old valet hitting on me?' I'd feel bad, but it's really kind of funny. If she only knew he was a prestigious dentist."

The woman seemed to do most of the talking, which meant that Jack probably didn't tell her the situation. She touched his shoulder as she turned toward the hotel's entrance. Jack and the others were not subtle in the way they ogled her. Jack watched the doors close behind her, smiled at us through the window and went back to work.

About ten minutes later, the blonde came back outside. She got Jack's attention and handed him something. He shook his head and slid it into his tight pocket. After she was safely back inside, Jack whipped out the object and held it up for us to see. She had given him her room key and a fifty-dollar bill.

Sam motioned him to come to the bar and got on her walkie-talkie. "James, tell the guys out front that Brad is done for the night. The party's over, so I think two valets are enough. Oh, and who's the blonde that just got another key from the desk?"

James's voice came back over the radio. "That's Jennifer Lance. She's in the Harvey Milk suite."

"Okay, have a bottle of Dom sent to her room, compliments of the valets."

"Um, okay. Whatever you say."

Jack pulled a chair up to our table and loosened his collar. He practically fell into his seat, clearly exhausted from all the running. "Damn, did you see her?"

"What did she say?" I asked.

"She just gave me her key, told me which suite and said she'd be awake until one. I wasn't sure if it was an invitation or if she was telling me her itinerary."

Sam smiled. "Fifty bucks. That's gotta be an invitation."

"Well, I'd like to think I'm worth more than fifty. Who is she?"

"All we know is that her name is Jennifer Lance. She didn't tell you more?" Sam finished her margarita.

"No. The other guys said she stays here a few times a year but doesn't linger much. She's always coming and going and usually gets back around eleven."

"I bet she's a drag queen." I laughed and noticed that Jack didn't find that remark amusing.

"Nah, probably married to some old fart with a gold mine and bad heart."

"She's alone at a hotel on Thanksgiving eve, she's not married. I'd have to guess she's here on business."

"What kind of business keeps you out until eleven?" I asked, fascinated.

"Maybe she dines clients. Maybe she's an escort." Sam laughed.

"Hell, I'm gonna go shower and find out. Don't wait up for me, ladies." Jack stood.

"Oh, we sent champagne to the room. Are you gonna tell her you're a dentist named Jack?"

"Actually, I think for tonight, I'm Brad . . . the oldest living valet."

"Night, Brad." We called in unison as he walked away.

"Think he'll get lucky?" Sam asked.

"If she's not a drag queen." I couldn't wait to hear the details.

It was nice to sleep in on Thanksgiving morning and not have to be up at five to stuff a bird. Sam was snoring away next to me. She'd ended up dealing with the cleaning staff until two a.m., trying to get the main dining room ready for the day's event. Between the alcohol and exhaustion, I never even heard her come in. I wasn't sure if Jack came in to his adjoining room after his big adventure. The clock read 7:52 and light was peeking in from behind the velvet curtains.

I heard the TV on in the room next door, so I lightly tapped on the connecting door.

"Come in." A raspy voice came from the other side.

"Are you decent?" I peeked my head in with my eyes closed.

"As decent as a boy named Brad can be for fifty bucks."

I pushed open the door and bounced over to his bed. "Oh, my. Tell me all the details."

"Nothing to tell, really." He reached to the bedside table and poured me a cup of coffee.

"Oh, come on. Something happened. Make something up if you have to."

"I let myself into her suite. She was sitting at the desk with a sketch pad and told me to come on in. She offered me a glass of champagne and told me to take a seat." He sipped his coffee and took a bite of a Danish. "Umm, these are great pastries."

"Yeah, yeah, they're wonderful. Then what?"

"Then she told me she's an artist. She asked if I would pose for her. She liked my build and my eyes." He batted his eyelashes.

"Pose? She gave you fifty bucks to pose?" I nearly choked on my coffee.

"No, she gave me three hundred to pose. But I didn't take it. I fessed up about being a dentist and told her that the pose was free."

"So, no wild story, no sex, no drag queen with a nightly show till eleven?"

"She had a gallery opening. She is featured at one of the galleries here and has a show a few times a year. She's really very good, I think. I told her we'd come by tomorrow and see her work."

"What did she say about your being a Dallas dentist?"

"She thought it was funny. She was relieved that a man my age wasn't a valet. She's a really nice lady. She has a son in college and a daughter in grade school. Her husband died two years ago."

"Any sparks? Any chance you'll keep in touch? A woman that looks that good should be kept in touch with."

"No. I think she really wants to be left alone. She did say that she'd have a copy of the sketch sent to the room sometime today."

"Well, I guess posing for an artist is better than a one-night stand." I was nonetheless a bit disappointed.

"I don't know about that, Doc. I wouldn't have minded a night of unbridled passion with a beautiful stranger."

"You and me both," I joked.

Jack and I spent the morning riding trolleys and window-shopping. Sam would meet us at one for turkey, then we were going to go for a drive and hit some bars. When we got back to the hotel, it was packed. I couldn't believe the number of people who'd decided to have their turkey at the Laine instead of cooking it themselves. The hotel staff was running around like, well, turkeys with their heads cut off. Jack and I took it upon ourselves to mingle with the guests and keep them comfortable as they waited to be seated.

Finally, we made it to our own table and Sam was able to join us. She sat down and handed Jack an envelope. "Your new friend left this for you at the front desk. She checked out this morning."

"Yeah, she's flying home to be with her kids." He took the envelope.

"So . . . how does it look?" I tried to sneak a peek.

"It's great. Amazing. She really is good." He slid it back inside the envelope. "I'll have to have it framed."

"Oh, come on, Jack. Let me see." I grabbed the envelope and he let go. I pulled the drawing out and took a long look. I didn't know how to react. I was viewing an amazing piece of art, a picture of my muscular brother and his huge . . . "Wow, is there such thing as poetic license in the art world?" I held the drawing up for Sam to view.

"Nope." Jack sighed. "That's all me, Doc. Your brother's hung like a mule." He rubbed his nails on his chest.

"Oh, my God." Sam was undoubtedly shocked.

"Oh, it's not that big." I laughed.

"No, they told me last night her name is Jennifer Lance. This is signed J.P. Lance."

Jack nodded. "Yeah. Jennifer Paige Lance. That's her name."

"I didn't put the two together. Jack, you posed for one of the greatest artists of our time. You know that mural in the new tower in Dallas?"

"Yeah. The one with all the children in it?"

"That's the one. Did you know they paid the artist one point two million to do that mural?"

"Damn. That's a lot of paint." Jack grinned.

"Yeah. That's J.P. Lance. Congrats, Jack. You should be honored." Sam patted his shoulder.

"You were in the presence of greatness." I smiled.

"So was she." Jack pointed to his crotch and giggled.

Thanksgiving came and went with great ease. There was none of that family drama that we all dreaded once a year. I never felt closer to my brother, and I thanked God that we lived close to each other. It broke my heart to leave Sam. I wasn't going to see her again for a while since I was heading north over Christmas break for Amy's memorial and the holiday. As much as I knew I should take Sam with me for the service, I also knew it wouldn't be the right time to come out to my parents. She said she understood, and I hoped she really did. We might get to spend New Year's together, but everything was up in the air. I was just happy to have spent the day with Sam and Jack. I knew, without a doubt, what I was grateful for on that Thanksgiving.

Chapter Eighteen

The house was still mostly unfurnished as per our deal. The lack of Sam's presence made it seem even emptier. I did take the time to hang Christmas lights and even got a little tree to remind myself what time of year it was. I was torn between pain and excitement about heading north for the holidays. I was really dreading the inevitable emotions I would feel during Amy's memorial. But I was looking forward to the snow and an old-fashioned family Christmas.

Jack and I thought about driving, but we worried about the weather and couldn't afford to be snowed in. The service was supposed to be in early December, but we had to postpone it because of my job and my mom's emergency hip surgery. Everyone agreed that December twentieth was a good day for it, although we did feel bad about pushing it so close to Christmas. Jack and I flew out the afternoon of the eighteenth with Amy's ashes packed in my carry-on. We had a three-hour layover in Denver, then a two-hour flight on a ten-seater plane to Gillette, followed by a three-hour drive up to our parents' house in the mountains of Wyoming. By the time we were finally on their doorstep, it was after midnight.

My parents were already in bed, so Jack and I settled in by the fire and helped ourselves to some of our old man's Scotch. I was exhausted but knew that sleep wouldn't come for a few hours. We went through old photo albums and didn't speak much about anything. I think we were both afraid to even say Amy's name for fear it would make the emptiness feel even greater. I stared out the window and watched the snow fall. I don't ever remember feeling so small and cold in my life. The warmth of the fire and the strength of my big brother's embrace weren't enough to make me feel secure. All I could think of was Sam. I longed to call her, but it was so late, and honestly, I didn't want a call to California to show up on my parents' phone bill. Damn lack of cell service in the mountains. I drank a second glass of Scotch in hopes it would either make the pain go away or put me to sleep. I think it did both, as I awoke hung over early the next morning with no recollection of falling to sleep on the sofa.

We had a lot of last-minute arrangements. Jack and I were sent the twenty miles to town to pay the printer and florist. We stopped off for lunch and ran into a lot of old friends. I had forgotten how small a place it was, where we grew up. Everyone shared their condolences and a thoughtful story about our sister. It felt really good being around people who knew and loved her. Her high-school boyfriend was driven to tears at the sight of me, and I had forgotten what a shock it must be for people to see me, looking so much like Amy. We secured rooms at the hotel for relatives and Amy's friends from Billings. The weather looked promising for their two-hour drive south to our small Wyoming town.

By the afternoon of the nineteenth, everything was in place for the service. A sort of wake was planned that night at the local watering hole. When we arrived, I sneaked off to a pay phone to call Sammy. She was waiting for my call and seemed relieved to hear my voice. I told her the details of the last two days and she filled me in on what was happening in her world. The distance between us seemed like a million miles. Her big elaborate hotel life made my hometown reunion seem so very small. The conversation seemed forced and I kept hoping for some deep words of advice to get me through the next twenty-four hours. No advice was given, no comforting words that I could hear. Later that night I would realize how much that simple "I love you" we exchanged would really mean to me.

I hung up the phone and found my way to the main bar area. I was awed by the huge number of people who had made their way up the mountain that night. It seemed like a high-school reunion and family reunion all in one. I saw old teachers, former employers, cousins, great uncles, neighbors—even the postmistress was in attendance. Our old Brownie troop was huddled by the fire. I fully expected to see them making s'mores and telling ghost stories. Jack's ex-girlfriend was there with her husband and three teenaged sons. My ex-husband and his pregnant wife even made the journey from Dallas. People had come from all over, some from as far away as Hawaii and Florida. The little airport must have been packed the last few days.

I didn't know what to say when people remarked about how much Amy and I looked alike. I had never met most of her Montana friends, and I think a few of them were haunted by my appearance. Jack held my hand throughout the evening, and every time I thought I was going to lose it, I felt him squeeze a little tighter. As trite as it sounds, there was a lot of love in that room that night, and it was a remarkable testimonial to the impact Amy had on the world.

As I lay in bed that night, dizzy from reliving all the conversations, a voice popped into my head. The voice of Sam was sweet enough to drown out every thought running through my cluttered mind. I knew that her voice was home to me and I let her words echo over and over until I drifted off to sleep: *I love you, Dani. I love you, Dani. I love you, Dani . . .*

It snowed the morning of December twentieth, although it didn't really seem cold enough to snow. The sun was trying hard to show itself as the huge wet flakes dropped from the sky and landed on the soft blanket of existing white. I had spent seven months writing the eulogy for Amy's service. As I read it over that morning, it just didn't seem good enough. I looked at my black wool suit and wool overcoat, and they just didn't seem good enough either. I glanced at the urn I had chosen for Amy's ashes, and like everything else, it just didn't seem good enough. I realized that nothing was good enough to pay tribute to a woman like Amy.

Jack and my parents were seated in silence at the kitchen table. I had always been the clown of the family and fought the urge to try and make them laugh. I poured a glass of orange juice and sat down in the same chair I always sat in as a child. A lump came to my throat as I glanced at Amy's empty childhood chair. One at a time, they each made eye contact with me, and I wondered if my presence—my appearance—was making them miss Amy even more.

"I can't change the way I look," I whispered and immediately started crying.

My mother got up and put her arms around me. "Oh, oh, sweetie. We don't want you to change the way you look. You have always been you. I've always seen you and Amy as individuals. You're a happy reminder, not a sad one. Don't cry, Danielle. Someone sent you flowers. Look. Roses." She motioned toward a beautiful porcelain vase filled with red and white flowers.

"Who sent them?" My face was still nestled in my mom's shoulder.

"I don't know. I didn't open the card. They sure are beautiful, though. I'm surprised they didn't send them to the service."

"I think those are for Dani personally, Mom. Probably not for the whole family, and probably none of our business." Jack tried, but his remark made my mother curious.

I went over and read the card. I knew who they were from, but I also knew she wouldn't sign her name or write anything incriminating, so I read the card aloud. "Danielle, our thoughts are with you today and always." It was signed simply, "Friends in Dallas."

"That was very nice. You have generous friends, Dani." My dad smiled.

"I have a wonderful community back home." I winked at Jack.

"Well, you seem to be well liked. I'm happy for you, Danielle. You and Amy always were the popular ones." Mom smiled as if she were bragging about herself.

I had no idea what to say in return, so I reached over and gave her a bear hug. She squeezed me so tight I thought I would break. Jack finally had to take over my end of the hug so I could get in the shower. I resisted the urge to call my "Friends in Dallas"—Sam and Kitty.

The town's only church was packed to the rafters by the time my family and I arrived. I was touched to see the beautiful array of flowers and more touched to see the dozens of somber faces. Jack and my parents took their seats in the front pews, and I slowly made my way to the front of the dimly lit church and stood behind the pulpit. We elected to keep this casual—no preacher—just a few words from me and anyone else who wanted to speak.

I felt at home in the church. It was where my family spent an occasional Sunday and religious holidays when we were kids. I always admired the majestic stained glass. I thought to myself how important it was to have stained glass in a place of worship. I figured windows were a good escape route for all the sins and a good entrance for all the salvation. I was never a religious person, but something about being in a church that morning—that particular church—gave me a sense of complacency and peace. I tried to look around at the faces in front of me, but it was too painful, so I stared at my notes and waited for my cue to begin.

"I had seven months to prepare what I was going to say today," I began, "but this morning I was afraid that what I wrote wasn't good enough. How do you pay tribute to someone as incredible as Amy? How do you express what you felt for her, or what her life meant to so many people?" I looked around the packed room and took a deep breath. I knew if I paused too long, or lingered on any faces, I would lose it. "Amy was my best friend from the moment I took my first breath. Every moment of my childhood was spent with her by my side. As adults, we went in different directions in life, but we always remained close. I could tell you stories—oh, Lord, do I have stories—of my adventures with that girl. But you aren't here today to hear my memories. You're here today to pay tribute to the kindest, sweetest woman you ever met." The only sound I could hear was the beating of my heart. "When Amy found out that the cancer was terminal, she wasn't worried. She told me that she had made peace with herself, and with the world. She said her only regret was that she wouldn't ever get to see another Super Bowl." My hands began shaking as I heard a few laughs from the crowd. "She said that she was happy with the way she had lived her life, that she had done everything she had dreamed of doing. I wonder how many of us can actually say that about ourselves. I thought about Amy's accomplishments in her short life, and it is a truly amazing list."

I felt a little dizzy and two people came up and stood next to me.

I recovered and continued. "Amy was our valedictorian, and after graduating from the University of Wyoming at age twenty-one, she went on to get her M.B.A. Before opening her travel agency, she made a point to travel the world. She said she couldn't send someone to Greece if she had never been there herself. She sent me postcards from every continent. She attended a wedding in Africa, a concert in Amsterdam, and won a jackpot in Monte Carlo. She funded her trips by giving tours and assistance to American travelers in other countries, amazing since she only spoke one language. When she returned to the States and decided to settle down, she chose Billings because she said it was as good a place as anywhere else in the world. 'It has an airport, good people and clean air . . . what more does one need?' she'd say. Her agency did well, and she was happy. That was the thing about Amy. She was always happy. I can't think of a day in my life where Sunshine Amy wasn't smiling and loving life."

The last word caught me off-guard. I felt someone take my hand and I did my best to keep going.

"I just know in my heart that Amy's journeys haven't ended. I know she's somewhere right now experiencing new things and making new friends. I just hope wherever she is, she can still feel my love, and the love that all of us have for her still, today and always."

I tried my best to continue, but the lump in my throat got the best of me. I was led to a seat and looked over at my family. Jack was inconsolable, but my parents showed no emotion. I realized it was my ex-husband, Steven, and his wife who had stood with me and led me to my seat. I wasn't sure how that made me feel, or if that was even appropriate, but I appreciated it nonetheless. A few other people got up and spoke. I'm not really sure I heard what they said, but I made it through the service.

That night, the four of us spread Amy's ashes over the canyon in a blizzard. It was peaceful, watching the snow fall and seeing her ashes blow away in the wind. I knew that she was on her way to places unknown, to new adventures. More important, I felt a sense of serenity, knowing that we had brought Amy home. At that moment I knew it was time for me to go home and start my own adventure with the other love of my life.

Chapter Nineteen

Jules and Sarah sat on their front porch and watched the New Year's Eve parade march by. There were only a few floats and one band, but it was a pretty good parade for a college town that lacked a football team. They had become great friends and had grown even closer without the pressure of romance. Sarah had gone on a few dates, while Jules went back to hiding behind her books. They knew they couldn't live together forever, but for the time being, it was the best solution for both of them.

"Got any big plans tonight?" Sarah grabbed a piece of candy that a clown threw on the porch.

"Nah. Just a night like all the others. You have plans?"

"I thought about going to Dallas, but I'm sure it's a madhouse. You know, all the gay folk trying to get in that midnight kiss."

"Well, I'd be willing to give it a try if you still want to go."

Jules watched a Shriner ride by on a moped.

"I'd like to go. It might be fun. Maybe you'll meet the love of your life down there." Sarah was being coy.

"I'm not looking to meet anyone, I just don't have anything else going on. But if you meet someone, give me a signal and I'll find a ride home."

"I'm not looking to meet anyone either, Jules."

They were quiet for a while, staring blankly at the street, even though the short parade had ended already.

"Sarah, suppose I could get a kiss at midnight?"

"I could go for that. It's bad luck to ring in the new year without a kiss."

"Is that a fact? Bad luck, eh?" Jules smiled.

"Well, I don't know if it's a fact, but I'd hate to risk it."

"Sarah, do you—" Jules stopped, regretting starting the question.

"Do I what?"

"Do you still fantasize about other women?"

"No. I don't fantasize anymore."

"Why do you suppose that is?" Jules couldn't help but smile.

Sarah took a deep breath and sat up straight. "Because I realized that I don't need to fantasize about someone I've already had sex with. I have the memories to replay as I lay awake at night."

"Memories of whom?" Jules prayed she was right in her assumption.

"Memories of you, Jules. You're the one that I want. I was just too stupid to appreciate what we had. I'd kill to be with you. If you'd have me."

"I'd have you." Jules didn't know what else to say.

"Shall we start over with that midnight kiss then?"

"There's nothing in the world I'd like more."

❧

Sam and I were able to be together for New Year's Eve after all. She adjusted her plans, negotiated deals with her employees and basically sold her soul to her father to get one night away from the hotel business. We lucked out and found an empty cabin at a lodge in Santa Fe. I didn't want to attend a loud party, and she didn't want to be in any town where there was a Laine Hotel. It made sense to find a cozy little retreat in the woods to hide out from the rest of the world, if only for one night.

I checked in at the lodge a few hours before Sam arrived. I felt like I hadn't slept in weeks, between the Thanksgiving trip, the trip north and this little jaunt. I took a long bath, lit the fireplace and fell asleep watching some soap opera I'd never heard of. I felt a sense of warmth when I awoke and saw that the fire was still blazing. Next to the bed, I saw Sam's suitcase, and curled up in a ball on my left, the beautiful Samantha Lynn Laine.

"Hey, stranger." I placed my hand on her hip. "How long have you been here?"

"About an hour. You were snoring away, so I took a shower and fed the fire."

"What time is it?"

"Who cares. For once, we don't have places to be, people to meet or things to worry about."

"When are you coming home to stay?"

"Just a few more weeks. Think you can wait that long?" She rested her head on my shoulder.

"I've waited my whole life to live with you. A few more weeks is cake."

"Mmm. Cake. Are you hungry?"

"A little. I'm more lonely than anything. Do you have a kiss for a tired old woman?"

"No, but I have a kiss for you—my beautiful, young dreamer." She leaned up and let her lips brush lightly against mine.

"So, do you have good news for me?"

"Yes, baby. I took the job at the law firm in Dallas. You knew I would . . ."

"It's a great firm, Sam. I'm really happy for you."

"I didn't take the job because of the firm. I took the job to be close to home."

"You sure love Dallas, huh?"

"I said I wanted to be close to home. If you're in Dallas, then Dallas is my home, Doc."

We had a romantic dinner at the lodge and made snow angels on a hillside. We were back at the cabin long before midnight, and we made the most of our precious time together. We talked about things we had never talked about. We told stories of our youth and laughed at our childish mistakes. She told me that all she wanted in the world was to settle down with me and spend a life together being happy. I still to this day have never understood what Sam sees in me, but I knew even then I wasn't going to let her go.

As midnight approached, we opened a bottle of champagne and headed outside. The stars were so bright, you could see forever. I took a long look at Sam and realized that in her eyes I could see forever. When the clock struck twelve, we kissed, made a toast and danced in the moonlight.

Visit

Spinsters Ink

at

SpinstersInk.com

or call our toll-free number

1-800-301-6860

Publications from Spinsters Ink

P.O. Box 242
Midway, Florida 32343
Phone: 800-301-6860
www.spinstersink.com

MERMAID by Michelene Esposito. When May unearths a box in her missing sister's closet she is taken on a journey through her mother's past that leads her not only to Kate but to the choices and compromises, emptiness and fullness, the beauty and jagged pain of love that all women must face.   ISBN 978-1-883523-85-5 $14.95

ASSISTED LIVING by Sheila Ortiz Taylor. Violet March, an eighty-two year old resident of Casa de los Sueños, finally has the opportunity to put years of mystery reading to practical use. One by one her comrades, the Bingos, are dying. Is this natural attrition, or is there a plot afoot?   ISBN 978-1-883523-84-2 $14.95

NIGHT DIVING by Michelene Esposito. *Night Diving* is both a young woman's coming-out story and a 30-something coming-of-age journey that proves you can go home again.
                ISBN 978-1-883523-52-7 $14.95

FURTHEST FROM THE GATE by Ann Roberts. *Furthest from the Gate* is a humorous chronicle of a woman's coming of age, her complicated relationship with her mother and the responsibilities to family that last a lifetime.   ISBN 978-1-883523-81-7 $14.95

EYES OF GRAY by Dani O'Connor. Grayson Thomas was the typical college senior with typical friends, a typical job and typical insecurities about her future. One Sunday morning, Gray's life became a little less typical, she saw a man clad in black, and started doubting her own sanity.   ISBN 978-1-883523-82-4 $14.95

ORDINARY FURIES by Linda Morgenstein. Tired of hiding, exhausted by her grief after her husband's death, Alexis Pope plunges into the refreshingly frantic world of restaurant resort cooking and dining in the funky chic town of Guerneville, California.
ISBN 978-1-883523-83-1 $14.95

A POEM FOR WHAT'S HER NAME by Dani O'Connor. Professor Dani O'Connor had pretty much resigned herself to the fact that there was no such thing as a complete woman. Then out of nowhere, along comes a woman who blows Dani's theory right out of the water.
ISBN 1-883523-78-8 $14.95

WOMEN'S STUDIES by Julia Watts. With humor and heart, *Women's Studies* follows one school year in the lives of three young women and shows that in college, one's extracurricular activities are often much more educational than what goes on in the classroom.
ISBN 1-883523-75-3 $14.95

THE SECRET KEEPING by Francine Saint Marie. *The Secret Keeping* is a high-stakes, girl-gets-girl romance, where the moral of the story is that money can buy you love if it's invested wisely.
ISBN 1-883523-77-X $14.95

DISORDERLY ATTACHMENTS by Jennifer L. Jordan. The fifth Kristin Ashe Mystery. Kris investigates whether a mansion someone wants to convert into condos is haunted.   ISBN 1-883523-74-5 $14.95

VERA'S STILL POINT by Ruth Perkinson. Vera is reminded of exactly what it is that she has been missing in life.
ISBN 1-883523-73-7 $14.95

OUTRAGEOUS by Sheila Ortiz-Taylor. Arden Benbow, a motorcycle riding, lesbian Latina poet from LA is hired to teach poetry in a small liberal arts college in Northwest Florida. ISBN 1-883523-72-9 $14.95

UNBREAKABLE by Blayne Cooper. The bonds of love and friendship can be as strong as steel. But are they unbreakable?
ISBN 1-883523-76-1 $14.95

ALL BETS OFF by Jaime Clevenger. Bette Lawrence is about to find out how hard life can be for someone of low society standing in the 1900s. ISBN 1-883523-71-0 $14.95

UNBEARABLE LOSSES by Jennifer L. Jordan. The fourth Kristin Ashe Mystery . Two elderly sisters have hired Kris to discover who is pilfering from their award-winning holiday display.
ISBN 1-883523-68-0 $14.95

FRENCH POSTCARDS by Jane Merchant. When Elinor moves to France with her husband and two children, she never expects that her life is about to be changed forever. ISBN 1-883523-67-2 $14.95

EXISTING SOLUTIONS by Jennifer L. Jordan. The second Kristin Ashe Mystery. When Kris is hired to find an activist's biological father, things get complicated when she finds herself falling for her client.
ISBN 1-883523-69-9 $14.95

A SAFE PLACE TO SLEEP by Jennifer L. Jordan. The first Kristin Ashe Mystery. Kris is approached by well-known lesbian Destiny Greaves with an unusual request. One that will lead Kris to hunt for her own missing childhood pieces. ISBN 1-883523-70-2 $14.95

Visit

Spinsters Ink

at

SpinstersInk.com

or call our toll-free number

1-800-301-6860